THE SHOOTING SCRIPT

THE SHAWSHANK REDEMPTION

THE SHAWSHANK REDEMPTION

SCREENPLAY AND NOTES BY

FRANK DARABONT

INTRODUCTION BY

STEPHEN KING

A Newmarket Shooting Script Series Book

NEWMARKET PRESS • NEW YORK

This book published simultaneously in the United States of America and in Canada.

96 97 98 99   10 9 8 7 6 5 4 3 2 1

Library of Congress Cataloging-in-Publication Data
Darabont, Frank.
The shawshank redemption: the shooting script/
screenplay and notes by Frank Darabont; introduction by Stephen King.
p. cm. — (A Newmarket screenplay)
ISBN 1-55704-246-2
1. Shawshank redemption (Motion picture) 2. King, Stephen, 1947– . Different Seasons or
Rita Hayworth and Shawshank Redemption. 3. King, Stephen, 1947– . —Film and video adaptations.
I. King, Stephen, 1947– . II. Title. III. Series.
PN1997.S433D37 1995
791.43' 72—dc20

95-33698
CIP

Quantity Purchases
Companies, professional groups, clubs, and other organizations may qualify for
special terms when ordering quantities of this title. For information, write to
Special Sales, Newmarket Press, 18 East 48th Street, New York, NY 10017, or call (212) 832-3575.

Book design by Tania Garcia.
Manufactured in the United States of America.

First Edition

OTHER NEWMARKET MOVIEBOOKS INCLUDE

For Allen…

*This published screenplay, as was the movie, is dedicated to
Allen Greene—gentleman, friend, and the only agent I ever met
willing to represent new screenwriters with no track records
whatsoever and invest the considerable time and effort needed to
build their careers from scratch. Without him, I might still be
nailing sets together for a living.*

*All author's proceeds from the sale of this
book will be donated to AIDS research and charities in his memory.*

CONTENTS

RITA HAYWORTH AND THE DARABONT REDEMPTION
by Stephen King

I love the movies.

When people ask how come so many films have been made from my work (twenty-five or so, including half a dozen pretty good ones), I say it's simple: I love the movies. From time to time I have been accused by curmudgeonly critics of writing with the movies foremost in my mind, but why would I? The money for the books is three times better…if, that is, money is even the yardstick we must use to measure with. The fact is, I have never written with the movies in mind, but I have *always* written with them in my *eye*. When asked why I had been so successful as a novelist, Bill Thompson, my first editor, said: "Steve has a projector in his head." I don't (it would be very bulky, for one thing, and would make it impossible to get through airport metal detectors), but sometimes it does feel that way. My books are the movies I see in my head, that's all. I write them down, and some producer says, "Hey! This'd make a pretty good movie!" because in a way it already *is* one.

I have loved the movies ever since my first one. Picture a little boy in short pants, already wearing glasses, sitting in the fifth row and staring gape-jawed at the giant cartoon images of *Bambi*. His hands are knotted in his crotch, this little boy, because he badly needs to go to the bathroom but won't ask his mother to take him; he can't bear to be away from those images even for that long. I loved the movies then, and still do now (although, at forty-seven, I tend to take more bathroom breaks). Around 1977 or so, when I started having some popular success, I saw a way to give back a little of the joy the movies had given me.

'77 was the year young filmmakers—college students, for the most part—started writing me about the stories I'd published (first in *Night Shift*, later in *Skeleton Crew*), wanting to make short films out of them. Over the objections of my accountant, who saw all sorts of possible legal problems, I established a policy which still holds today. I will grant any student filmmaker the right to make a movie out of any short story I have written (*not* the novels, that would be ridiculous), so long as the film rights are still mine to assign. I ask them to sign a paper promising that no resulting film will be exhibited commercially without my approval, and that they send me a videotape of the finished work. For this one-time right I ask a dollar. I have made the dollar-deal, as I call it, over my accountant's moans and head-clutching protests sixteen or seventeen times as of this writing. Stories filmed include "Night Surf," "The Boogeyman," and "Last Rung on the Ladder" from *Night Shift*, "Cain Rose Up" and "Here There Be Tygers" from *Skeleton Crew*, and a fairly impressive eighteen-minute version of "The Sun Dog" from *Four Past Midnight*. Many of these adaptations weren't so great, but a few showed at least a smattering of talent. Talent or lack of it rarely made any difference to me, however; I was trying to pay back a little of what I'd been given over the years—hours of happiness in the dark. So I'd look at the films (usually alone and usually just once; in many cases one viewing was all a person could bear), then put them up on a shelf I had marked Dollar Babies.

The only time things took a different course was in the case of Frank Darabont, a twenty-year-old filmmaker who wrote and asked to make a film out of a *Night Shift* story called "The Woman in the Room." The request seemed surpassingly odd to me on the face of it, because "Woman" was very unlike most of the other stories in *Night Shift*. It had been written as a kind of cry from the heart after my mother's long, losing battle with cervical cancer had finally ended. Her pain—the *pointlessness* of her pain—shook me in a deep and fundamental way; it made me see the world in a new and cautious perspective. That was in addition to the natural grief almost anyone feels when a parent dies at the relatively young age of sixty-two.

I granted young Mr. Darabont's request, however, and noted in passing that he was only one of two filmmakers who had ever been in touch with me who didn't write like an almost total illiterate (the other guy also made a pretty good short film, by the way). Darabont's check for one dollar turned up in the mail, and I forgot about him.

Three years later, in 1983, I remembered in a hurry. Frank sent me a videocassette of his film, and I watched it in slack-jawed amazement. I also felt a little sting of tears. *The Woman in the Room* remains, twelve years later, on my short list of favorite film adaptations. If you want to see why, you may be able to find a rental cassette still kicking around in your local video store (probably mis-shelved in the horror section). It's apt to be paired with Jeff Schiro's not uninteresting short film of "The Boogeyman."

Frank won an award for *Woman*, he and I exchanged a number of pleasant letters, and then we went back to our separate lives. He tracked mine through my books, I imagine, and I tracked him through his occasional screen credit for things like *The Blob* remake and *The Fly* sequel.

Then—around 1987, according to the man himself—Frank wrote and asked if he could option one of the novellas from *Different Seasons*, a prison-break story in the grainy old Warner Brothers/Jimmy Cagney mold. It came with the clunky, unlikely monicker of *Rita Hayworth and Shawshank Redemption*. I told Frank sure, almost casually. I never in a million years thought he would get the film made, but I had no qualms about granting him an option—based on *The Woman in the Room*, I knew that if his longshot *did* come in and the film *did* get made, it would probably turn out to be something interesting, even if it arrived broken.

Besides, I wanted to see what sort of screenplay he could *possibly* generate for the story, which has plenty of visual elements but is—on the whole—a lot less visual than novels such as *Firestarter* (one of my most visual novels and a resounding failure as a film). *Shawshank Redemption* actually owes a lot to Max Brand, who wrote the "Dr. Kildare" novels and a number of wonderful Westerns back in the '40s. Brand had a trick of having his plain-spun narrators say, "I want to tell you about this amazing friend of mine," and then telling you—all modest and unaware—about himself. I had always loved this technique of creating a hero out of a secondary character (sort of like turning Watson into Sherlock Holmes), and determined to try it with *Shawshank Redemption*. The result was a moody tale with more thinking than action in it…not the sort of thing that usually makes a good movie.

What I should have remembered, however, is that it *is* the sort of thing that, every now and then, makes a *great* movie.

So where was I? Okay, the option deal. We did that part, and five years or so went by. During that time, Frank directed a kickass cable movie called *Buried Alive* (the USA Network, I think), but otherwise I almost lost sight of him. I assumed that he was either having trouble with the screenplay or had given it up as a bad job. Then, one day in 1992, this fucking *huge* screenplay arrived from Monsieur Darabont. I mean this baby looked almost as big as the novella itself. I didn't open it at first, just sat in my office chair balancing it on my hand and thinking, "No way, Frank, baby. I don't even have to open it to know no one in their right mind is going to make a movie out of *this* leviathan. It'd translate into a film as long as the director's cut of *1900*."

I eventually put these gloomy thoughts aside and read it, though. It was great— too great, I thought, to be produced by any company in California. I did not feel there was a place for *Rita Hayworth and Shawshank Redemption* in an industry consumed with Predators and Terminators and cops whose best lines were "Yippie-ki-yay, motherfucker." Still, I renewed Frank's option (I guess; I don't think I ever exactly cashed the second check) and sent him onward with my blessing.

And behold, he found Castle Rock, which had been founded on an unlikely success associated with my work: Rob Reiner's funky, joyful version of "The Body." That story, also from *Different Seasons*, became *Stand By Me*, and made lots of bucks. In the years since, Castle Rock Pictures has more or less rescued my film-associated reputation from the scrap-heap, and no picture had more to do with that than the one which eventually became known as *The Shawshank Redemption* (not, as the critics so liberally pointed out, the best title ever conceived, but what the fuck were you going to call it? *Sybil Danning's Ass Catches Fire*? Sybil Danning wasn't even *in* the damned thing). As I write this, *Shawshank* has been nominated for seven Academy Awards, including Best Picture (Frank himself was cruelly and inexplicably left out as Best Director, God knows why), and may actually win some. Seems unlikely, but hey! In a world where a guy like Buster Douglas can knock out a guy like Mike Tyson, anything's possible, right?

Besides, the little gold statues aren't the point here; you have to remember that several of those statues were once won by a picture in which Paul Newman rode a funny bicycle while B. J. Thomas sang "Raindrops Keep Fallin' on My Head." The point is that sometimes talent still shines even under the most strenuous and adverse circumstances. As someone who has been *in* the film world but not *of* it ever since Paul Monash optioned my book *Carrie* in 1974, I enjoy a rather unique perspective…and from that perspective, I can tell you there was no way Frank should ever have been allowed to make his version of my novella, and no way his vision should ever have survived intact if he *was* given the chance. And yet it happened; almost every word and motion of the screenplay I balanced on my hand and dismissed by virtue of its very *weight* exists on film. Hoary old devices that should not work—Morgan Freeman's ubiquitous voice-overs, for instance—have been brushed off and somehow, by virtue of the filmmaker's craft and love, made to shine again. The actors give great performances, and for once, the film's length seems a blessing rather than a curse.

Frank's screenplay follows. I urge you to read it and enjoy it, but also to marvel over it: you are, in the realest sense, reading a dream come true, a miraculous triumph of art over the buck. As for me, I'm just grateful to have known Frank, and to have experienced the Darabont Redemption firsthand.

March 1995
Bangor, Maine

STEPHEN KING AND THE DARABONT REDEMPTION
by Frank Darabont

I love the movies too.

For me it wasn't *Bambi,* though; for me it was *Robinson Crusoe on Mars,* a cheesy-but-charming science fiction retelling of the Defoe adventure classic, starring Paul Mantee as Commander "Kit" Draper (the Crusoe role), Victor Lundin as Friday, and Barney the Woolly Monkey as Mona, the spacefaring simian mascot. (Adam West, pre-*Batman,* makes a brief appearance early in the film.) I was five years old, and it was the first movie I ever saw in an honest-to-god *real* movie theater. My brother Andy—a whole eight years older, and impossibly wise and beneficent in my eyes—had decided to treat his annoying squirt of a sibling to a matinee showing, so he perched me on the handlebars of his bike and pedaled us all the way to the World Theater (now long-shuttered) on Hollywood Boulevard. It was a distance of maybe three miles, but the trip he took me on that day might as well have been three million light-years. The events that unfolded as if by spontaneous magic in that darkened movie theater blew my mind; it was like nothing I'd ever seen or imagined before. It was a *movie.* Not wimpy black-and-white phosphor-dots flickering on a television tube, but full-color images thundering on a huge reflective screen. It commanded attention. *Sit there and listen,* it said. *This is not a place for idle viewing, this is a place of worship.*

From there, I embarked on a childhood watching everything I could clap my eyeballs on. I reveled in the Universal monster flicks. I rejoiced at the George Pal movies. I wallowed in Ray Harryhausen effects spectaculars. I fell on the detonator plunger with Alec Guinness, blowing up the bridge that spanned the River Kwai. I went on a journey beyond time and space with a computer named Hal. I went back and saw *The Omega Man* a dozen times. I soaked up every potboiler and grade Z melodrama I could stay up late enough to watch…

…but it wasn't *just* movies. It was also books. Stories and more stories, wonders for the taking, adventures galore. I could never seem to get enough of great storytellers growing up, and I still can't. In my lexicon of master yarn-spinners are names like Ray Bradbury, Mark Twain, Richard Matheson, Harlan Ellison, Charles Dickens, Shirley Jackson, Edgar Allan Poe, Saki, Raymond Chandler…

…oh, and a guy named Steve King.

I first stumbled across his work by sheer happy accident when I was in high school. I had joined a book-of-the-month club because their come-on was simply too tempting to resist—you got to order five books for a dime (or something like that), after which you had a few years to buy a certain number of books at regular cost. Every month or so they'd send you another pamphlet describing all the books you could choose, along with a main selection—the tricky part being, if you *didn't* want the main selection automatically shipped to you, you had to remember to mail the card back to them.

I seldom had the money to buy a new book, even at low book club prices, so I almost always sent the card back. But every once in a while I'd be a scatterbrained teenager and forget. And sure enough, much to my dismay, a book I hadn't meant to order would arrive in the mail. Filled with remorse and riddled with temptation, I'd open the box and pull the book out long enough to at least glance at it and flip a few pages—but lacking the funds to buy, I'd inevitably repackage it and ship it back unread…

…with *one* exception. I recall getting this one particular book with a vaguely ominous cover. *Looks kinda cool,* I remember thinking, *but I still can't afford it.* As I was reaching to put it back in the box for return shipment, I idly flipped the pages open and here's what I saw: *The woman in the tub had been dead for a long time. She was bloated and purple, her gas-filled belly rising out of the cold, ice-rimmed water like some fleshy island. Her eyes were fixed on Danny's, glassy and huge, like marbles. She was grinning, her purple lips pulled back in a grimace. Her breasts lolled. Her pubic hair floated. Her hands were frozen on the knurled porcelain sides of the tub like crab claws.*

Got *my* attention, you bet. I put any thought of returning the book momentarily on hold; I had to read on. I skimmed a swell paragraph detailing young Danny's horrified reaction to the rotted corpse he's discovered, and then the author nailed me with the kicker of the scene, a simple line that read: *The woman was sitting up.*

That did it. No way was I gonna send *that* book back! I'd have to scrape the money together somehow. I read it—no, *consumed* it—in one sitting, unable to tear my eyes from the pages. Anybody who remembers reading *The Shining* for the first time will know what I'm talking about.

From there I backtracked and read King's two earlier works, *Carrie* and *Salem's Lot*. Man, I was hooked. I became another of his growing legion of fans, grabbing anything with his name on it as soon as it hit the shelves. Not just the bestsellers, but *everything.* That's how I discovered his wrenching short story "The Woman in the Room," which my friends and I spent three years making as a short film. And that's also how I came across a gem of a short novel called *Rita Hayworth and Shawshank Redemption,* which told the tall and gentle tale of a decades-long friendship between two inmates in a fictional Maine prison. It was a story that captured my imagination and sent my heart soaring. It also instilled in me the hope that, someday, I might be lucky enough to put it on film.

It's funny, but until I read his introduction to this book, I never really knew exactly *why* Steve ever granted me the rights to either *The Woman in the Room* or *The Shawshank Redemption.* Now we *all* know, and it's just as I suspected—Steve is simply a nice guy. You can believe him when he says he wants to give something back. The man walks it like he talks it. I'm living proof of that.

Every once in a while, if we're lucky, somebody comes into our lives and helps us along. If this help is consistent and meaningful, that person eventually assumes Patron Saint status. In my life, though he may not have even intended it, Stephen King has become such a person. Though I can never hope to repay the many kindnesses he's shown me, I do take deep pleasure in the satisfaction he felt at seeing *The Shawshank Redemption* up there on the big screen for the very first time. He thought the movie treated his story well, which means a lot to me. And maybe that's enough; maybe making a movie he likes from a story I loved is my way of giving back to *him.* Being a nice guy who loves the movies, that's probably all he ever wanted. Still, I can't pass up the opportunity to embarrass him with my thanks, so here goes:

Thanks, Steve. Thanks for letting me borrow a little of your storytelling mojo. Thanks for coming into my life and helping me along. Thanks for giving back.

■

I had a specific reason for doing this book. I often get letters from people, mostly high school or college age, seeking advice on how to become a screenwriter. I'm no expert, but I guess I *am* a screenwriter, so I try to answer as many of these as I can. The advice I give is fairly consistent, and I'd like to print excerpts from three of my response letters here for the benefit of those who are of a similar mind:

> "...if it's any consolation in your efforts to write, please know that we all battle the usual feelings of frustration and insecurity, regardless of age or experience. For me, writing has always been a process of working through my self-doubt, which is ever present. I'd be lying if I didn't admit that writing can be one of the most self-tormenting occupations one can choose, and for the sim-

plest of reasons: if one cares about the work, if aiming high and stretching is a personal goal, then writing becomes a constant exercise in seeking the limits of one's own abilities. That's a good thing, certainly, but the perverse downside of seeking one's limits is that one usually finds them, which is akin to running headlong and unhelmeted into a brick wall on a daily basis. The good news is, every time you smack into it, that wall gets pushed a little further back—inches at a time, mind you, but it does move. That's why it's important not to give in to your fears and doubts, and to keep writing..."

"*...my best recommendation is to write. Endlessly to write. This is the oldest but most valuable bit of advice in the world. It amazes me when somebody talks about wanting to sell a screenplay without actually having written before, which is akin to deciding you're a carpenter without ever having hammered a nail into wood, or thinking you're ready to join an orchestra without ever having practiced a musical instrument. I guess movies are so accessible that people figure writing one doesn't require any special skill, that anybody can do it, but it's not true. As with any skill, it requires work. The more you work, the more you sharpen and develop your talent. That, coupled with a staggering amount of determination and persistence, might get you somewhere...*"

"*...I'm impressed with your reasoning in trying to get your hands on some screenplays. You're right, it is important to see the difference between what was written and what ended up on screen. More than that, it's important to see how a screenplay works, both in the physical layout as well as the subtler elements (character, theme, structure, etc.). I did the same thing when I was your age, although you have a distinct advantage in that screenplays are a lot easier to come by nowadays than they were back then (they weren't often sold when I was in high school, nor reprinted in books, both of which are now common practice). I found that reading scripts gave me a feel for how they work, and when asked for advice on becoming a screenwriter, I always recommend the same. In fact, I still read scripts of films I admire. A well-written screenplay always has something new to teach you, no matter how long you've been at it. I might suggest an excellent book,* Best American Screenplays, *edited by Sam Thomas. It contains the shooting scripts of some terrific films, including* Butch Cassidy and the Sundance Kid *and* Casablanca...*"

Though I hope all three excerpts may hold some value for the aspiring writer, it's the third that perhaps best explains the philosophy behind this book. I've noticed an unfortunate trend in published screenplays lately, which is to *transcribe the finished film* and then pass it off as the script. It's what I call the "vanity"

approach. It's all beautifully typeset and lavishly illustrated, but there's one problem—
it isn't the screenplay. It doesn't look like one, read like one, or smell like one. It's dic-
tation. It's a coffee-table book. More to the point, I think it cheats the very
readership these books are meant to serve, the film students and movie buffs. Who
else but they buy published screenplays? Who else but they stand to gain the most
by comparing the original screenplay to the finished film?

The vanity approach drives me crazy because it doesn't tell us what we need to
know; it plays hide-and-go-seek with the truth. I far prefer the way Quentin
Tarantino's excellent *Pulp Fiction* screenplay was published in the first American edition—*as* written, warts and all. It's the script he and his actors walked onto the set
with every morning. It's not even *typeset;* the pages in the book are actual repro-
ductions of the pages that came out of his typewriter. Reading it gave me insight
into how the film was actually *made.* It showed me where scenes were tightened,
how things changed, what the actors brought to it…in other words, it taught me
something.

I'd like to give my heartfelt thanks to Esther Margolis—the fine lady who published the book you now hold in your hands—for allowing me the pleasure of letting you read my script in its original form. It's the one I wrote, the one Castle Rock
decided to make, the one my cast and crew dealt with every day. It hasn't been typeset to look prettier; the pages you see are those that came out of my computer's
printer. It's got plenty of warts on display—things that changed, locations that
shifted, entire scenes that aren't in the movie. Following the screenplay, you'll find
a section titled *Mutatis Mutandis,* which describes *why* things changed.

One last thing before I go. To fairly and completely trace the evolution of this
film from written word to movie screen, you really should start by reading Stephen
King's remarkable short novel, *Rita Hayworth and Shawshank Redemption.* That's
where it all started, and that's where it still lives.

April 1995
Los Angeles, CA

"THE SHAWSHANK REDEMPTION"

screenplay by
Frank Darabont

based on the novella
"Rita Hayworth and Shawshank Redemption"
by Stephen King

THIRD DRAFT (FINAL)
2/22/93

*Hope is a good thing, maybe the best of
things, and no good thing ever dies...*

1   INT - CABIN - NIGHT (1946)   1

A dark, empty room.

The door bursts open. A MAN and WOMAN enter, drunk and
giggling, horny as hell. No sooner is the door shut than
they're all over each other, ripping at clothes, pawing at
flesh, mouths locked together.

He gropes for a lamp, tries to turn it on, knocks it over
instead. Hell with it. He's got more urgent things to do, like
getting her blouse open and his hands on her breasts. She
arches, moaning, fumbling with his fly. He slams her against
the wall, ripping her skirt. We hear fabric tear.

He enters her right then and there, roughly, up against the
wall. She cries out, hitting her head against the wall but not
caring, grinding against him, clawing his back, shivering with
the sensations running through her. He carries her across the
room with her legs wrapped around him. They fall onto the bed.

CAMERA PULLS BACK, exiting through the window, traveling
smoothly outside...

2   EXT - CABIN - NIGHT (1946)   2

...to reveal the bungalow, remote in a wooded area, the
lovers' cries spilling into the night...

...and we drift down a wooded path, the sounds of rutting
passion growing fainter, mingling now with the night sounds of
crickets and hoot owls...

...and we begin to hear FAINT MUSIC in the woods, tinny and
incongruous, and still we keep PULLING BACK until...

...a car is revealed. A 1946 Plymouth. Parked in a clearing.

3   INT - PLYMOUTH - NIGHT (1946)   3

ANDY DUFRESNE, mid-20's, wire rim glasses, three-piece suit.
Under normal circumstances a respectable, solid citizen; hardly
dangerous, perhaps even meek. But these circumstances are far
from normal. He is disheveled, unshaven, and very drunk. A
cigarette smolders in his mouth. His eyes, flinty and hard, are
riveted to the bungalow up the path.

He can hear them fucking from here.

He raises a bottle of bourbon and knocks it back. The radio
plays softly, painfully romantic, taunting him:

> You stepped out of a dream...
> You are too wonderful...
> To be what you seem...

(CONTINUED)

3 CONTINUED   3

He opens the glove compartment, pulls out an object wrapped
in a rag. He lays it in his lap and unwraps it carefully --

-- revealing a .38 revolver. Oily, black, evil.

He grabs a box of bullets. Spills them everywhere, all over
the seats and floor. Clumsy. He picks bullets off his lap,
loading them into the gun, one by one, methodical and grim.
Six in the chamber. His gaze goes back to the bungalow.

He shuts off the radio. Abrupt silence, except for the distant
lovers' moans. He takes another shot of bourbon courage, then
opens the door and steps from the car.

4 EXT - PLYMOUTH - NIGHT (1946)   4

His wingtip shoes crunch on gravel. Loose bullets scatter to
the ground. The bourbon bottle drops and shatters.

He starts up the path, unsteady on his feet. The closer he
gets, the louder the lovemaking becomes. Louder and more
frenzied. The lovers are reaching a climax, their sounds of
passion degenerating into rhythmic gasps and grunts.

                    WOMAN (O.S.)
              Oh god...oh god...oh god...

Andy lurches to a stop, listening. The woman cries out in
orgasm. The sound slams into Andy's brain like an icepick. He
shuts his eyes tightly, wishing the sound would stop.

It finally does, dying away like a siren until all that's left
is the shallow gasping and panting of post-coitus. We hear
languorous laughter, moans of satisfaction.

                    WOMAN (O.S.)
              Oh god...that's sooo good...you're
              the best...the best I ever had...

Andy just stands and listens, devastated. He doesn't look like
much of a killer now; he's just a sad little man on a dirt
path in the woods, tears streaming down his face, a loaded gun
held loosely at his side. A pathetic figure, really.

FADE TO BLACK: 1ST TITLE UP

5 INT - COURTROOM - DAY (1946)   5

THE JURY listens like a gallery of mannequins on display,
pale-faced and stupefied.

                    D.A. (O.S.)
              Mr. Dufresne, describe the
              confrontation you had with your
              wife the night she was murdered.

                                                      (CONTINUED)

5 CONTINUED   5

ANDY DUFRESNE

is on the witness stand, hands folded, suit and tie pressed,
hair meticulously combed. He speaks in soft, measured tones:

                    ANDY
          It was very bitter. She said she
          was glad I knew, that she hated all
          the sneaking around. She said she
          wanted a divorce in Reno.

                    D.A.
          What was your response?

                    ANDY
          I told her I would not grant one.

                    D.A.
               (refers to his notes)
          "I'll see you in Hell before I see
          you in Reno." Those were the words
          you used, Mr. Dufresne, according
          to the testimony of your neighbors.

                    ANDY
          If they say so. I really don't
          remember. I was upset.

FADE TO BLACK: 2ND TITLE UP

                    D.A.
          What happened after you and your
          wife argued?

                    ANDY
          She packed a bag and went to stay
          with Mr. Quentin.

                    D.A.
          Glenn Quentin. The golf pro at the
          Falmouth Hills Country Club. The
          man you had recently discovered was
          her lover.
               (Andy nods)
          Did you follow her?

                    ANDY
          I went to a few bars first. Later,
          I decided to drive to Mr. Quentin's
          home and confront them. They
          weren't there...so I parked my car
          in the turnout...and waited.

                    D.A.
          With what intention?

                                        (CONTINUED)

                         ANDY
          I'm not sure. I was confused. Drunk.
          I think mostly I wanted to scare them.

                         D.A.
          You had a gun with you?

                         ANDY
          Yes. I did.

FADE TO BLACK: 3RD TITLE UP

                         D.A.
          When they arrived, you went up
          to the house and murdered them?

                         ANDY
          No. I was sobering up. I realized
          she wasn't worth it. I decided to
          let her have her quickie divorce.

                         D.A.
          Quickie divorce indeed. A .38
          caliber divorce, wrapped in a
          handtowel to muffle the shots,
          isn't that what you mean? And then
          you shot her lover!

                         ANDY
          I did not. I got back in the car
          and drove home to sleep it off.
          Along the way, I stopped and threw
          my gun into the Royal River. I feel
          I've been very clear on this point.

                         D.A.
          Yes, you have. Where I get hazy,
          though, is the part where the
          cleaning woman shows up the next
          morning and finds your wife and her
          lover in bed, riddled with .38
          caliber bullets. Does that strike
          you as a fantastic coincidence, Mr.
          Dufresne, or is it just me?

                         ANDY
                    (softly)
          Yes. It does.

                         D.A.
          I'm sorry, Mr. Dufresne, I don't
          think the jury heard that.

                         ANDY
          Yes. It does.

                                        (CONTINUED)

                              D.A.
          Does what?

                              ANDY
          Strike me as a fantastic coincidence.

                              D.A.
          On that, sir, we are in accord...

FADE TO BLACK: 4TH TITLE UP

                              D.A.
          You claim you threw your gun into
          the Royal River before the murders
          took place. That's rather convenient.

                              ANDY
          It's the truth.

                              D.A.
          You recall Lt. Mincher's testimony?
          He and his men dragged that river
          for three days and nary a gun was
          found. So no comparison can be made
          between your gun and the bullets
          taken from the bloodstained corpses
          of the victims. That's also rather
          convenient, isn't it, Mr. Dufresne?

                              ANDY
                    (faint, bitter smile)
          Since I am innocent of this crime,
          sir, I find it decidedly inconvenient
          the gun was never found.

FADE TO BLACK: 5TH TITLE UP

6   INT - COURTROOM - DAY (1946)   6

The D.A. holds the jury spellbound with his closing summation:

                              D.A.
          Ladies and gentlemen, you've heard
          all the evidence, you know all the
          facts. We have the accused at the
          scene of the crime. We have foot
          prints. Tire tracks. Bullets
          scattered on the ground which bear
          his fingerprints. A broken bourbon
          bottle, likewise with fingerprints.
          Most of all, we have a beautiful
          young woman and her lover lying
          dead in each other's arms. They had
          sinned. But was their crime so
          great as to merit a death sentence?

                                                        (CONTINUED)

6 CONTINUED   6

He gestures to Andy sitting quietly with his ATTORNEY.

> D.A.
> I suspect Mr. Dufresne's answer to that would be yes. I further suspect he carried out that sentence on the night of September 21st, this year of our Lord, 1946, by pumping four bullets into his wife and another four into Glenn Quentin. And while you think about that, think about this...

He picks up a revolver, spins the cylinder before their eyes like a carnival barker spinning a wheel of fortune.

> D.A.
> A revolver holds six bullets, not eight. I submit to you this was not a hot-blooded crime of passion! That could at least be understood, if not condoned. No, this was revenge of a much more brutal and cold-blooded nature. Consider! Four bullets per victim! Not six shots fired, but eight! That means he fired the gun empty...and then stopped to reload so he could shoot each of them again! An extra bullet per lover...right in the head.
> (a few JURORS shiver)
> I'm done talking. You people are all decent, God-fearing Christian folk. You know what to do.

FADE TO BLACK: 6TH TITLE UP

7   INT - JURY ROOM - DAY (1946)   7

CAMERA TRACKS down a long table, moving from one JUROR to the next. These decent, God-fearing Christians are chowing down on a nice fried chicken dinner provided them by the county, smacking greasy lips and gnawing cobbettes of corn.

> VOICE (O.S.)
> Guilty. Guilty. Guilty. Guilty...

We find the FOREMAN at the head of the table, sorting votes.

FADE TO BLACK: 7TH TITLE UP

8   INT - COURTROOM - DAY (1946)   8

Andy stands before the dias. THE JUDGE peers down, framed by a carved frieze of blind Lady Justice on the wall.

8

(CONTINUED)

8 CONTINUED   8

                              JUDGE
               You strike me as a particularly icy
               and remorseless man, Mr. Dufresne.
               It chills my blood just to look at
               you. By the power vested in me by
               the State of Maine, I hereby order
               you to serve two life sentences,
               back to back, one for each of your
               victims. So be it.

He raps his gavel as we

CRASH TO BLACK: LAST TITLE UP.

9   AN IRON-BARRED DOOR   9

slides open with an enormous CLANG. A stark room waits beyond.
CAMERA PUSHES through. SEVEN HUMORLESS MEN sit side by side at
a long table. An empty chair faces them. We are now in:

INT - SHAWSHANK HEARINGS ROOM - DAY (1947)

RED enters, removes his cap and waits by the chair.

                              MAN #1
               Sit.

Red sits, tries not to slouch. The chair is uncomfortable.

                              MAN #2
               We see by your file you've served
               twenty years of a life sentence.

                              MAN #3
               You feel you've been rehabilitated?

                              RED
               Yes, sir. Absolutely. I've learned
               my lesson. I can honestly say I'm a
               changed man. I'm no longer a danger
               to society. That's the God's honest
               truth. No doubt about it.

The men just stare at him. One stifles a yawn.

CLOSEUP - PAROLE FORM

A big rubber stamp slams down: "REJECTED" in red ink.

10   EXT - EXERCISE YARD - SHAWSHANK PRISON - DUSK (1947)   10

High stone walls topped with snaky concertina wire, set off at
intervals by looming guard towers. Over a hundred CONS are
in the yard. Playing catch, shooting craps, jawing at each
other, making deals. Exercise period.

(CONTINUED)

10 CONTINUED   10

RED emerges into fading daylight, slouches low-key through the
activity, worn cap on his head, exchanging hellos and doing
minor business. He's an important man here.

> RED (V.O.)
> There's a con like me in every prison
> in America, I guess. I'm the guy who
> can get it for you. Cigarettes, a
> bag of reefer if you're partial, a
> bottle of brandy to celebrate your
> kid's high school graduation. Damn
> near anything, within reason.

He slips somebody a pack of smokes, smooth sleight-of-hand.

> RED (V.O.)
> Yes sir, I'm a regular Sears &
> Roebuck.

TWO SHORT SIREN BLASTS issue from the main tower, drawing
everybody's attention to the loading dock. The outer gate
swings open...revealing a gray prison bus outside.

> RED (V.O.)
> So when Andy Dufresne came to me in
> 1949 and asked me to smuggle Rita
> Hayworth into the prison for him, I
> told him no problem. And it wasn't.

> CON
> Fresh fish! Fresh fish today!

Red is joined by HEYWOOD, SKEET, FLOYD, JIGGER, ERNIE, SNOOZE.
Most cons crowd to the fence to gawk and jeer, but Red and his
group mount the bleachers and settle in comfortably.

11   INT - PRISON BUS - DUSK (1947)   11

Andy sits in back, wearing steel collar and chains.

> RED (V.O.)
> Andy came to Shawshank Prison in
> early 1947 for murdering his wife
> and the fella she was bangin'.

The bus lurches forward, RUMBLES through the gates. Andy gazes
around, swallowed by prison walls.

> RED (V.O.)
> On the outside, he'd been vice-
> president of a large Portland bank.
> Good work for a man as young as he
> was, when you consider how
> conservative banks were back then.

12   EXT - PRISON YARD - DUSK (1947)   12

                        TOWER GUARD
              All clear!

GUARDS approach the bus with carbines. The door jerks open.
The new fish disembark, chained together single-file, blinking
sourly at their surroundings. Andy stumbles against the MAN in
front of him, almost drags him down.

BYRON HADLEY, captain of the guard, slams his baton into
Andy's back. Andy goes to his knees, gasping in pain. JEERS
and SHOUTS from the spectators.

                        HADLEY
              On your feet before I fuck you up
              so bad you never walk again.

13   ON THE BLEACHERS   13

                        RED
              There they are, boys. The Human
              Charm Bracelet.

                        HEYWOOD
              Never seen such a sorry-lookin'
              heap of maggot shit in my life.

                        JIGGER
              Comin' from you, Heywood, you being
              so pretty and all...

                        FLOYD
              Takin' bets today, Red?

                        RED
                  (pulls notepad and pencil)
              Bear Catholic? Pope shit in the woods?
              Smokes or coin, bettor's choice.

                        FLOYD
              Smokes. Put me down for two.

                        RED
              High roller. Who's your horse?

                        FLOYD
              That gangly sack of shit, third
              from the front. He'll be the first.

                        HEYWOOD
              Bullshit. I'll take that action.

                        ERNIE
              Me too.

(CONTINUED)

Other hands go up. Red jots the names.

                    HEYWOOD
          You're out some smokes, son. Take
          my word.

                    FLOYD
          You're so smart, you call it.

                    HEYWOOD
          I say that chubby fat-ass...let's
          see...<u>fifth</u> from the front. Put me
          down for a quarter deck.

                    RED
          That's five cigarettes on Fat-Ass.
          Any takers?

More hands go up. Andy and the others are paraded along,
forced by their chains to take tiny baby steps, flinching
under the barrage of jeers and shouts. The old-timers are
shaking the fence, trying to make the newcomers shit their
pants. Some of the new fish shout back, but mostly they look
terrified. Especially Andy.

                    RED (V.O.)
          I must admit I didn't think much of
          Andy first time I laid eyes on him.
          He might'a been important on the
          outside, but in here he was just a
          little turd in prison grays. Looked
          like a stiff breeze could blow him
          over. That was my first impression
          of the man.

                    SKEET
          What say, Red?

                    RED
          Little fella on the end. Definitely.
          I stake half a pack. Any takers?

                    SNOOZE
          Rich bet.

                    RED
          C'mon, boys, who's gonna prove me
          wrong?
                    (hands go up)
          Floyd, Skeet, Joe, Heywood. Four brave
          souls, ten smokes apiece. That's it,
          gentlemen, this window's closed.

Red pockets his notepad. A VOICE comes over the P.A. speakers:

                              VOICE (amplified)
                    Return to your cellblocks for
                    evening count.

14   INT - ADMITTING AREA - DUSK (1947)   14

     The new fish are marched in. Guards unlock the shackles. The
     chains drop away, rattling to the stone floor.

                              HADLEY
                    Eyes front.

     WARDEN SAMUEL NORTON strolls forth, a colorless man in a gray
     suit and a church pin in his lapel. He looks like he could
     piss ice water. He appraises the newcomers with flinty eyes.

                              NORTON
                    This is Mr. Hadley, captain of the
                    guard. I am Mr. Norton, the warden.
                    You are sinners and scum, that's
                    why they sent you to me. Rule
                    number one: no blaspheming. I'll
                    not have the Lord's name taken in
                    vain in my prison. The other rules
                    you'll figure out as you go along.
                    Any questions?

                              CON
                    When do we eat?

     Cued by Norton's glance, Hadley steps up to the con and screams
     right in his face:

                              HADLEY
                    YOU EAT WHEN WE SAY YOU EAT! YOU
                    PISS WHEN WE SAY YOU PISS! YOU SHIT
                    WHEN WE SAY YOU SHIT! YOU SLEEP
                    WHEN WE SAY YOU SLEEP! YOU MAGGOT-
                    DICK MOTHERFUCKER!

     Hadley rams the tip of his club into the con's belly. The
     man falls to his knees, gasping and clutching himself.
     Hadley takes his place at Norton's side again. Softly:

                              NORTON
                    Any other questions?
                         (there are none)
                    I believe in two things. Discipline
                    and the Bible. Here, you'll receive
                    both.
                         (holds up a Bible)
                    Put your faith in the Lord. Your
                    ass belongs to me. Welcome to
                    Shawshank.

(CONTINUED)

                                HADLEY
                Off with them clothes! And I didn't
                say take all day doing it, did I?

The men shed their clothes. Within seconds, all stand naked.

                                HADLEY
                First man into the shower!

Hadley shoves the FIRST CON into a steel cage open at the
front. TWO GUARDS open up with a fire hose. The con is slammed
against the back of the cage, sputtering and hollering.
Seconds later, the water is cut and the con yanked out.

                                HADLEY
                Delouse that piece of shit! Next
                man in!

The con gets a huge scoop of white delousing powder thrown all
over him. Gasping and coughing, blinking powder from his eyes,
he gets shoved to a trustee's cage. The TRUSTEE slides a short
stack of items through the slot -- prison clothes and a Bible.
All the men are processed quickly -- a blast of water, powder,
clothes and a Bible...

15   INT - INFIRMARY - NIGHT (1947)   15

A naked CON steps before a DOCTOR and gets a cursory exam.
A penlight is shined in his eyes, ears, nose, and throat.

                                DOCTOR
                Bend over.

The con does. A GUARD with a penlight in his teeth spreads his
cheeks, peers up his ass, and nods. Andy is next up. He gets
the same treatment.

16   INT - PRISON CHAPEL - NIGHT (1947)   16

CAMERA TRACKS the naked newcomers shivering on hard wooden
chairs, clothes on their laps, Bibles open.

                                CHAPLAIN (O.S.)
                ...maketh me to lie down in green
                pastures. He leadeth me beside the
                still waters. He restoreth my soul...

17   INT - CELLBLOCK FIVE - NIGHT (1947)   17

Three tiers to a side, concrete and steel, gray and imposing.
Andy and the others are marched in, still naked, carrying
their clothes and Bibles. The CONS in their cells greet them
with TAUNTS, JEERS, and LAUGHTER. One by one, the new men are
shown to their cells and locked in with a CLANG OF STEEL.

>   RED (V.O.)
> The first night's the toughest, no
> doubt about it. They march you in
> naked as the day you're born, fresh
> from a Bible reading, skin burning
> and half-blind from that delousing
> shit they throw on you...

Red watches from his cell, arms slung over the crossbars,
cigarette dangling from his fingers.

>   RED (V.O.)
> ...and when they put you in that
> cell, when those bars slam home,
> that's when you know it's for real.
> Old life blown away in the blink of
> an eye...a long cold season in hell
> stretching out ahead...nothing
> left but all the time in the world
> to think about it.

Red listens to the CLANGING below. He watches Andy and a few
others being brought up to the 2nd tier.

>   RED (V.O.)
> Most new fish come close to madness
> the first night. Somebody always
> breaks down crying. Happens every
> time. The only question is, who's
> it gonna be?

Andy is led past and given a cell at the end of the tier.

>   RED (V.O.)
> It's as good a thing to bet on as
> any, I guess. I had my money on
> Andy Dufresne...

18   INT - ANDY'S CELL - NIGHT (1947)   18

The bars slam home. Andy is alone in his cell, clutching his
clothes. He gazes around at his new surroundings, taking it
in. He slowly begins to dress himself...

19   EXT - SHAWSHANK PRISON - NIGHT (1947)   19

A malignant stone growth on the Maine landscape. The moon
hangs low and baleful in a dead sky. The headlight of a
PASSING TRAIN cuts through the night.

20   INT - RED'S CELL - NIGHT (1947)   20

Red lies on his bunk below us, tossing his baseball toward the
ceiling and catching it again. He pauses, listening. FOOTSTEPS
approach below, unhurried, echoing hollowly on stone.

21   INT - CELLBLOCK FIVE - NIGHT (1947)   21

LOW ANGLE. A CELLBLOCK GUARD strolls into frame.

                         GUARD
          That's <u>lights</u> <u>out!</u> Good night, ladies.

The lights bump off in sequence. The guard exits, footsteps
echoing away. Darkness now. Silence. CAMERA CRANES UP the
tiers toward Red's cell.

                         RED (V.O.)
          I remember my first night. Seems a
          long time ago now.

Red looms from the darkness, leans on the bars. Listens.
Waits. From somewhere below comes faint, ghastly tittering.
VOICES drift through the cellblock, taunting:

                         VARIOUS VOICES (O.S.)
          Fishee fishee fisheeee...You're
          gonna like it here, new fish. A
          <u>whooole</u> lot...Make you wish your
          daddies never dicked your
          mommies...You takin' this down, new
          fish? Gonna be a quiz later.
                    (somebody LAUGHS)
          Sshhh. Keep it down. The screws'll
          hear...Fishee fishee fisheeee...

                         RED (V.O.)
          The boys always go fishin' with
          first-timers...and they don't quit
          till they reel someone in.

The VOICES keep on, sly and creepy in the dark...

22   INT - VARIOUS CELLS - NIGHT (1947)   22
thru   thru 25
25   ...while the new cons go quietly crazy in their cells. One man
      paces like a caged animal...another sits gnawing his cuticles
      bloody...a third is weeping silently...a fourth is dry-heaving
      into the toilet...

26   INT - RED'S CELL - NIGHT (1947)   26

Red waits at the bars. Smoking. Listening. He cranes his head,
peers down toward Andy's cell. Nothing. Not a peep.

                         HEYWOOD (O.S.)
          Fat-Ass...oh, Faaaat-Ass. Talk to
          me, boy. I know you're in there. I
          can hear you breathin'. Now don't
          you lissen to these nitwits, hear?

27   INT - FAT-ASS' CELL - NIGHT (1947)   27

Fat-Ass is crying, trying not to hyperventilate.

                    HEYWOOD (O.S.)
          This ain't such a bad place. I'll
          introduce you around, make you feel
          right at home. I know some big ol'
          bull queers who'd <u>love</u> to make your
          acquaintance...especially that big
          white mushy butt of yours...

And that's it. Fat-Ass lets out a LOUD WAIL of despair:

                    FAT-ASS
          OH GOD! I DON'T BELONG HERE! I
          WANNA GO HOME!

28   INT - HEYWOOD'S CELL - NIGHT (1947)   28

                    HEYWOOD
          AND IT'S FAT-ASS BY A NOSE!

29   INT - CELLBLOCK - NIGHT (1947)   29

The place goes nuts. Fat-Ass throws himself screaming against
the bars. The entire block starts CHANTING:

                    VOICES
          Fresh <u>fish</u>...fresh <u>fish</u>...fresh
          <u>fish</u>...fresh <u>fish</u>...

                    FAT-ASS
          I WANNA GO HOME! I WANT MY MOTHER!

                    VOICE (O.S.)
          I <u>had</u> your mother! She wasn't that
          great!

The lights bump on. GUARDS pour in, led by Hadley himself.

                    HADLEY
          What the Christ is this happy shit?

                    VOICE (O.S.)
          He took the Lord's name in vain!
          I'm tellin' the warden!

                    HADLEY
                 (to the unseen wit)
          You'll be tellin' him with my baton
          up your ass!

Hadley arrives at Fat-Ass' cell, bellowing through the bars:

(CONTINUED)

29 CONTINUED   29

> HADLEY
> What's your malfunction you fat
> fuckin' barrel of monkey-spunk?

> FAT-ASS
> PLEASE! THIS AIN'T RIGHT! I AIN'T
> SUPPOSED TO BE HERE! NOT ME!

> HADLEY
> I ain't gonna count to three! Not
> even to one! Now shut the fuck up
> 'fore I sing you a lullabye!

Fat-Ass keeps blubbering and wailing. Total freak-out. Hadley
draws his baton, gestures to his men. Open it.

A GUARD unlocks the cell. Hadley pulls Fat-Ass out and starts
beating him with the baton, brutally raining blows. Fat-Ass
falls, tries to crawl.

The place goes dead silent. All we hear now is the dull
THWACK-THWACK-THWACK of the baton. Fat-ass passes out. Hadley
gets in a few more licks and finally stops.

> HADLEY
> Get this tub of shit down to the
> infirmary.
>   (peers around)
> If I hear so much as a mouse fart
> in here the rest of the night, by
> God and Sonny Jesus, you'll all
> visit the infirmary. Every last
> motherfucker here.

The guards wrestle Fat-Ass onto a stretcher and carry him off.
FOOTSTEPS echo away. Lights off. Darkness again. Silence.

30   INT - RED'S CELL - NIGHT (1947)   30

Red stares through the bars at the main floor below, eyes
riveted to the small puddle of blood where Fat-Ass went down.

> RED (V.O.)
> His first night in the joint, Andy
> Dufresne cost me two packs of
> cigarettes. He never made a sound...

31   INT - CELLBLOCK FIVE - MORNING (1947)   31

LOUD BUZZER. The master locks are thrown -- KA-THUMP! The cons
step from their cells, lining the tiers. The GUARDS holler
their head-counts to the HEAD BULL, who jots on a clipboard.
Red peers at Andy, checking him out. Andy stands in line,
collar buttoned, hair combed.

32   INT - MESS HALL - MORNING (1947)   32

Andy goes through the breakfast line, gets a scoop of glop on
his tray. WE PAN ANDY through the noise and confusion...and
discover BOGS DIAMOND and ROOSTER MacBRIDE watching Andy go
by. Bogs sizes Andy up with a salacious gleam in his eye,
mutters something to Rooster. Rooster laughs.

Andy finds a table occupied by Red and his regulars, chooses
a spot at the end where nobody is sitting. Ignoring their
stares, he picks up his spoon -- and pauses, seeing something
in his food. He carefully fishes it out with his fingers.

It's a squirming maggot. Andy grimaces, unsure what to do with
it. BROOKS HATLEN is sitting closest to Andy. At age 65, he's
a senior citizen, a long-standing resident.

                         BROOKS
              You gonna eat that?

                         ANDY
              Hadn't planned on it.

                         BROOKS
              You mind?

Andy passes the maggot to Brooks. Brooks examines it, rolling
it between his fingertips like a man checking out a fine
cigar. Andy is riveted with apprehension.

                         BROOKS
              Mmm. Nice and ripe.

Andy can't bear to watch. Brooks opens up his sweater and
feeds the maggot to a baby crow nestled in an inside pocket.
Andy breathes a sigh of relief.

                         BROOKS
              Jake says thanks. Fell out of his
              nest over by the plate shop. I'm
              lookin' after him till he's old
              enough to fly.

Andy nods, proceeds to eat. Carefully. Heywood approaches.

                         JIGGER
              Oh, Christ, here he comes.

                         HEYWOOD
              Mornin', boys. It's a **fine** mornin'.
              You know **why** it's fine?

Heywood plops his tray down, sits. The men start pulling out
cigarettes and handing them down.

(CONTINUED)

32 CONTINUED   32

                         HEYWOOD
               That's right, send 'em all down. I
               wanna see 'em lined up in a row,
               pretty as a chorus line.

An impressive pile forms. Heywood bends down and inhales
deeply, smelling the aroma. Rapture.

                         FLOYD
               Smell my ass...

                         HEYWOOD
               Gee, Red. Terrible shame, your
               horse comin' in last and all.
               Hell, I sure do love that horse of
               mine. I believe I owe that boy a
               big sloppy kiss when I see him.

                         RED
               Give him some'a your cigarettes
               instead, cheap bastard.

                         HEYWOOD
               Say Tyrell, you pull infirmary duty
               this week? How's that winnin' horse
               of mine, anyway?

                         TYRELL
               Dead.
                    (the men fall silent)
               Hadley busted his head pretty good.
               Doc already went home for the
               night. Poor bastard lay there till
               this morning. By then...

He shakes his head, turns back to his food. The silence
mounts. Heywood glances around. Men resume eating. Softly:

                         ANDY
               What was his name?

                         HEYWOOD
               What? What'd you say?

                         ANDY
               I was wondering if anyone knew his
               name.

                         HEYWOOD
               What the fuck you care, new fish?
                    (resumes eating)
               Doesn't matter what his fuckin'
               name was. He's dead.

33   INT - PRISON LAUNDRY - DAY (1947)   33

A DEAFENING NOISE of industrial washers and presses. Andy works
the laundry line. A nightmarish job. He's new at it. BOB, the
con foreman, elbows him aside and shows him how it's done.

34   INT - SHOWERS - DAY (1947)   34

Shower heads mounted in bare concrete. Andy showers with a
dozen or more men. No modesty here. At least the water is good
and hot, soothing his tortured muscles.

Bogs looms from the billowing steam, smiling, checking Andy up
and down. Rooster and PETE appear from the sides. The Sisters.

                        BOGS
              You're some sweet punk. You been
              broke in yet?

Andy tries to step past them. He gets shoved around, nothing
serious, just some slap and tickle. Jackals sizing up prey.

                        BOGS
              Hard to get. I like that.

Andy breaks free, flushed and shaking. He hurries off, leaving
the three Sisters laughing.

35   INT - ANDY'S CELL - NIGHT (1947)   35

Andy lies staring at the darkness, unable to sleep.

36   EXT - EXERCISE YARD - DAY (1947)   36

Exercise period. Red plays catch with Heywood and Jigger,
lazily tossing a baseball around. Red notices Andy off to the
side. Nods hello. Andy takes this as a cue to amble over.
Heywood and Jigger pause, watching.

                        ANDY
                  (offers his hand)
              Hello. I'm Andy Dufresne.

Red glances at the hand, ignores it. The game continues.

                        RED
              The wife-killin' banker.

                        ANDY
              How do you know that?

                        RED
              I keep my ear to the ground. Why'd
              you do it?

                        21   (CONTINUED)

                         ANDY
              I didn't, since you ask.

                         RED
              Hell, you'll fit right in, then.
                    (off Andy's look)
              Everyone's innocent in here, don't
              you know that? Heywood! What are
              you in for, boy?

                         HEYWOOD
              Didn't do it! Lawyer fucked me!

Red gives Andy a look. See?

                         ANDY
              What else have you heard?

                         RED
              People say you're a cold fish. They
              say you think your shit smells
              sweeter than ordinary. That true?

                         ANDY
              What do you think?

                         RED
              Ain't made up my mind yet.

Heywood nudges Jigger. Watch this. He winds up and throws the
ball hard -- right at Andy's head. Andy sees it coming out of
the corner of his eye, whirls and catches it. Beat. He sends
the ball right back, zinging it into Heywood's hands. Heywood
drops the ball and grimaces, wringing his stung hands.

                         ANDY
              I understand you're a man who knows
              how to get things.

                         RED
              I'm known to locate certain things
              from time to time. They seem to
              fall into my hands. Maybe it's
              'cause I'm Irish.

                         ANDY
              I wonder if you could get me a
              rock-hammer?

                         RED
              What is it and why?

                         ANDY
              You make your customers' motives a
              part of your business?

                              RED
            If you wanted a toothbrush, I
            wouldn't ask questions. I'd just
            quote a price. A toothbrush, see,
            is a non-lethal sort of object.

                              ANDY
            Fair enough. A rock-hammer is about
            eight or nine inches long. Looks
            like a miniature pickaxe, with a
            small sharp pick on one end, and a
            blunt hammerhead on the other. It's
            for rocks.

                              RED
            Rocks.

Andy squats, motions Red to join him. Andy grabs a handful of
dirt and sifts it through his hands. He finds a pebble and
rubs it clean. It has a nice milky glow. He tosses it to Red.

                              RED
            Quartz?

                              ANDY
            Quartz, sure. And look. Mica. Shale.
            Silted granite. There's some graded
            limestone, from when they cut this
            place out of the hill.

                              RED
            So?

                              ANDY
            I'm a rockhound. At least I was, in
            my old life. I'd like to be again,
            on a limited scale.

                              RED
            Yeah, that or maybe plant your toy
            in somebody's skull?

                              ANDY
            I have no enemies here.

                              RED
            No? Just wait.

Red flicks his gaze past Andy. Bogs is watching them.

                              RED
            Word gets around. The Sisters have
            taken a real shine to you, yes they
            have. Especially Bogs.

(CONTINUED)

                         ANDY
          Tell me something. Would it help if
          I explained to them I'm not
          homosexual?

                         RED
          Neither are they. You have to be
          human first. They don't qualify.
                    (off Andy's look)
          Bull queers take by force, that's
          all they want or understand. I'd
          grow eyes in the back of my head if
          I were you.

                         ANDY
          Thanks for the advice.

                         RED
          That comes free. But you understand
          my concern.

                         ANDY
          If there's trouble, I doubt a rock-
          hammer will do me any good.

                         RED
          Then I guess you wanna escape.
          Tunnel under the wall maybe?
                    (Andy laughs politely)
          I miss the joke. What's so funny?

                         ANDY
          You'll know when you see the rock-
          hammer.

                         RED
          What's this item usually go for?

                         ANDY
          Seven dollars in any rock and gem shop.

                         RED
          My standard mark-up's twenty
          percent, but we're talkin' about a
          special object. Risk goes up, price
          goes up. Call it ten bucks even.

                         ANDY
          Ten it is.

                         RED
          I'll see what I can do.
                    (rises, slapping dust)
          But it's a waste of money.

36 CONTINUED   36

                          ANDY
              Oh?

                          RED
              Folks who run this place <u>love</u>
              surprise inspections. They turn a
              blind eye to some things, but not
              a gadget like that. They'll find
              it, and you'll lose it. Mention my
              name, we'll never do business
              again. Not for a pair of shoelaces
              or a stick of gum.

                          ANDY
              I understand. Thank you, Mr...?

                          RED
              Red. The name's Red.

                          ANDY
              Red. I'm Andy. Pleasure doing
              business with you.

They shake. Andy strolls off. Red watches him go.

                          RED (V.O.)
              I could see why some of the boys
              took him for snobby. He had a quiet
              way about him, a walk and a talk
              that just wasn't normal around
              here. He <u>strolled,</u> like a man in a
              park without a care or worry. Like
              he had on an invisible coat that
              would shield him from this place.
                      (resumes playing catch)
              Yes, I think it would be fair to
              say I liked Andy from the start.

37 INT - MESS HALL - DAY (1947)   37

Red gets his breakfast and heads for a table. Andy falls in
step, slips him a tightly-folded square of paper.

38 INT - RED'S CELL - NIGHT (1947)   38

Lying on his bunk, Red unfolds the square. A ten dollar bill.

                          RED (V.O.)
              He was a man who adapted fast.

39 EXT - LOADING DOCK - DAY (1947)   39

Under watchful supervision, CONS are off-loading bags of dirty
laundry from an "Eliot Nursing Home" truck.

(CONTINUED)

39 CONTINUED   39

> RED (V.O.)
> Years later, I found out he'd
> brought in quite a bit more than
> just ten dollars...

A certain bag hits the ground. The TRUCK DRIVER shoots a look
at a black con, LEONARD, then ambles over to a GUARD to shoot
the shit. Leonard loads the bag onto a cart...

40   INT - PRISON LAUNDRY - DAY (1947)   40

Bags are being unloaded. We find Leonard working the line.

> RED (V.O.)
> When they check you into this
> hotel, one of the bellhops bends
> you over and looks up your works,
> just to make sure you're not
> carrying anything. But a truly
> determined man can get an object
> quite a ways up there.

Leonard slips a small paper-wrapped package out of the laundry
bag, hides it under his apron, and keeps sorting...

41   INT - PRISON LAUNDRY EXCHANGE - DAY (1947)   41

Red deposits his dirty bundle and moves down the line to where
the clean sheets are being handed out.

> RED (V.O.)
> That's how Andy joined our happy
> little Shawshank family with more
> than five hundred dollars on his
> person. Determination.

Leonard catches Red's eye, turns and grabs a specific stack of
clean sheets. He hands it across to Red --

TIGHT ANGLE

-- and more than clean laundry changes hands. Two packs of
cigarettes slide out of Red's hand into Leonard's.

42   INT - RED'S CELL - DAY (1947)   42

Red slips the package out of his sheets, carefully checks to
make sure nobody's coming, then rips it open. He pulls out the
rock-hammer. It's just as Andy described. Red laughs softly.

> RED (V.O.)
> Andy was right. I finally got the
> joke. It would take a man about six
> hundred years to tunnel under the
> wall with one of these.

43   INT - CELLBLOCK FIVE - 2ND TIER - NIGHT (1947)   43

Brooks Hatlen pushes a cart of books from cell to cell. The
rolling library. He finds Red waiting for him. Red slips the
rock-hammer, wrapped in a towel, through the bars and onto the
cart. Next comes six cigarettes to pay for postage.

                              RED
                Dufresne.

Brooks nods, never missing a beat. He rolls his cart to
Andy's cell, mutters through the bars:

                            BROOKS
                Middle shelf, wrapped in a towel.

Andy's hand snakes through the bars and makes the object
disappear. The hand comes back and deposits a small slip of
folded paper along with more cigarettes. Brooks turns his cart
around and goes back. He pauses, sorting his books long enough
for Red to snag the slip of paper. Brooks continues on,
scooping the cigarettes off the cart and into his pocket.

44   INT - RED'S CELL - NIGHT (1947)   44

Red unfolds the slip of paper. Penciled neatly on it is a
single word: "Thanks."

45   INT - PRISON LAUNDRY - DAY (1947)   45

We are assaulted by the deafening noise of the laundry line.
Andy is doing his job, getting good at it.

                            BOB
                DUFRESNE! WE'RE LOW ON HEXLITE!
                HEAD ON BACK AND FETCH US UP SOME!

Andy nods. He leaves the line, weaving his way through the
laundry room and into --

46   INT - BACK ROOMS/STOCK AREA - DAY (1947)   46

-- a dark, tangled maze of rooms and corridors, boilers and
furnaces, sump pumps, old washing machines, pallets of
cleaning supplies and detergents, you name it. Andy hefts a
cardboard drum of Hexlite off the stack, turns around --

-- and finds Bogs Diamond in the aisle, blocking his way.
Rooster looms from the shadows to his right, Pete Verness
on the left. A frozen beat. Andy slams the Hexlite to the
floor, rips off the top, and scoops out a double handful.

                            ANDY
                You get this in your eyes, it
                blinds you.

                                              (CONTINUED)

46 CONTINUED   46

                                BOGS
                    Honey, hush.

Andy backs up, holding them at bay, trying to maneuver through
the maze. The Sisters keep coming, tense and guarded, eyes
riveted and gauging his every move, trying to outflank him.
Andy trips on some old paint supplies. That's all it takes.
They're on him in an instant, kicking and stomping.

Andy gets yanked to his feet. Bogs applies a chokehold from
behind. They propel him across the room and slam him against
an old four-pocket machine, bending him over it. Rooster jams
a rag into Andy's mouth and secures it with a steel pipe, like
a horse bit. Andy kicks and struggles, but Rooster and Pete
have his arms firmly pinned. Bogs whispers in Andy's ear:

                                BOGS
                    That's it, fight. Better that way.

Andy starts screaming, muffled by the rag. CAMERA PULLS BACK,
SLOWLY WIDENING. The big Washex blocks our view. All we see
is Andy's screaming face and the men holding him down...

...and CAMERA DRIFTS FROM THE ROOM, leaving the dark place
and the dingy act behind...MOVING up empty corridors, past
concrete walls and steel pipes...

                                RED (V.O.)
                    I wish I could tell you that Andy
                    fought the good fight, and the
                    Sisters let him be. I wish I could
                    tell you that, but prison is no
                    fairy-tale world.

WE EMERGE into the prison laundry past a guard, WIDENING for
a final view of the line. The giant steel "mangler" is
slapping down in brutal rhythm. The sound is deafening.

                                RED (V.O.)
                    He never said who did it...but we
                    all knew.

PRISON MONTAGE: (1947 through 1949)

47 Andy plods through his days. Working. Eating. Chipping and   47
    shaping his rocks after lights-out...

                                RED (V.O.)
                    Things went on like that for a
                    while. Prison life consists of
                    routine, and then more routine.

48 Andy walks the yard, face swollen and bruised.   48

(CONTINUED)

48 CONTINUED   48

                              RED (V.O.)
                    Every so often, Andy would show up
                    with fresh bruises.

49   Andy eats breakfast. A few tables over, Bogs blows him a kiss.   49

                              RED (V.O.)
                    The Sisters kept at him. Sometimes
                    he was able to fight them off...
                    sometimes not.

50   Andy backs into a corner in some dingy part of the prison,   50
     wildly swinging a rake at his tormentors.

                              RED (V.O.)
                    He always fought, that's what I
                    remember. He fought because he knew
                    if he didn't fight, it would make
                    it that much easier not to fight
                    the next time.

     The rake connects, snapping off over somebody's skull. They
     beat the hell out of him.

                              RED (V.O.)
                    Half the time it landed him in the
                    infirmary...

51   INT - SOLITARY CONFINEMENT ("THE HOLE") - NIGHT (1949)   51

     A stone closet. No bed, sink, or lights. Just a toilet with no
     seat. Andy sits on bare concrete, bruised face lit by a faint
     ray of light falling through the tiny slit in the steel door.

                              RED (V.O.)
                    ...the other half, it landed him in
                    solitary. Warden Norton's "grain &
                    drain" vacation. Bread, water, and
                    all the privacy you could want.

52   INT - PRISON LAUNDRY - DAY (1949)   52

     Andy is working the line.

                              RED (V.O.)
                    And that's how it went for Andy. That
                    was his routine. I do believe those
                    first two years were the worst for
                    him. And I also believe if things
                    had gone on that way, this place
                    would have got the best of him.
                    But then, in the spring of 1949,
                    the powers-that-be decided that...

53 EXT - PRISON YARD - DAY (1949)   53

Warden Norton addresses the assembled cons via bullhorn:

> NORTON
> ...the roof of the license-plate
> factory needs resurfacing. I need a
> dozen volunteers for a week's work.
> We're gonna be taking names in this
> steel bucket here...

Red glances around at his friends. Andy also catches his eye.

> RED (V.O.)
> It was outdoor detail, and May is
> one damn fine month to be workin'
> outdoors.

54 EXT - PRISON YARD - DAY (1949)   54

Cons shuffle past, dropping slips of paper into a bucket.

> RED (V.O.)
> More than a hundred men volunteered
> for the job.

Red saunters to a guard named TIM YOUNGBLOOD, mutters
discreetly in his ear.

55 EXT - PRISON YARD - DAY (1949)   55

Youngblood is pulling names and reading them off. Red
exchanges grins with Andy and the others.

> RED (V.O.)
> Wouldn't you know it? Me and some
> fellas I know were among the names
> called.

56 INT - PRISON CORRIDOR - NIGHT (1949)   56

Red slips Youngblood six packs of cigarettes.

> RED (V.O.)
> Only cost us a pack of smokes per
> man. I made my usual twenty
> percent, of course.

57 EXT - LICENSE PLATE FACTORY - DAY (1949)   57

A tar-cooker bubbles and smokes. TWO CONS dip up a bucket of
tar and tie a rope to the handle. The rope goes taught. CAMERA
FOLLOWS the bucket of tar up the side of the building to --

-- where it is relayed to the work detail. The men are dipping
big Padd brushes and spreading the tar. ANGLE OVER to Byron
Hadley bitching sourly to his fellow guards:

                         HADLEY
              ...so this shithead lawyer calls
              long distance from Texas, and he
              says, Byron Hadley? I say, yeah. He
              says, sorry to inform you, but your
              brother just died.

                         YOUNGBLOOD
              Damn, Byron. Sorry to hear that.

                         HADLEY
              I ain't. He was an asshole. Run off
              years ago, family ain't heard of him
              since. Figured him for dead anyway.
              So this lawyer prick says, your
              brother died a rich man. Oil wells
              and shit, close to a million bucks.
              Jesus, it's frigging incredible how
              lucky some assholes can get.

                         TROUT
              A million bucks? Jeez-Louise! You
              get any of that?

                         HADLEY
              Thirty five thousand. That's what
              he left me.

                         TROUT
              Dollars? Holy shit, that's great!
              Like winnin' a lottery...
                       (off Hadley's shitty look)
              ...ain't it?

                         HADLEY
              Dumbshit. What do you figger the
              government's gonna do to me? Take a
              big wet bite out of my ass, is what.

                         TROUT
              Oh. Hadn't thought of that.

                         HADLEY
              Maybe leave me enough to buy a new
              car with. Then what happens? You
              pay tax on the car. Repairs and
              maintenance. Goddamn kids pesterin'
              you to take 'em for a ride...

                                              (CONTINUED)

>   MERT
> And <u>drive</u> it, if they're old enough.

>   HADLEY
> That's right, wanting to drive it,
> wanting to <u>learn</u> on it, f'Chrissake!
> Then at the end of the year, if you
> figured the tax wrong, they make
> you pay out of your own pocket.
> Uncle Sam puts his hand in your
> shirt and squeezes your tit till
> it's purple. Always get the short
> end. That's a fact.
>   (spits over the side)
> Some brother. Shit.

The prisoners keep spreading tar, eyes on their work.

>   HEYWOOD
> Poor Byron. What terrible fuckin'
> luck. Imagine inheriting thirty
> five thousand dollars.

>   RED
> Crying shame. Some folks got it
> awful bad.

Red glances over -- and is shocked to see Andy standing up,
listening to the guards talk.

>   RED
> Hey, you nuts? Keep your eyes on
> your pail!

Andy tosses his Padd in the bucket and strolls toward Hadley.

>   RED
> Andy! Come back! Shit!

>   SNOOZE
> What's he <u>doing?</u>

>   FLOYD
> Gettin' himself killed.

>   RED
> God <u>damn</u> it...

>   HEYWOOD
> Just keep spreadin' tar...

The guards stiffen at Andy's approach. Youngblood's hand goes
to his holster. The tower guards CLICK-CLACK their rifle
bolts. Hadley turns, stupefied to find Andy there.

(CONTINUED)

58 CONTINUED

> ANDY
> Mr. Hadley. Do you trust your wife?

> HADLEY
> That's funny. You're gonna look
> funnier suckin' my dick with <u>no</u>
> <u>fuckin' teeth.</u>

> ANDY
> What I mean is, do you think she'd
> go behind your back? Try to
> hamstring you?

> HADLEY
> That's it! Step aside, Mert. This
> fucker's havin' hisself an accident.

Hadley grabs Andy's collar and propels him violently toward
the edge of the roof. The cons furiously keep spreading tar.

> HEYWOOD
> Oh God, he's gonna do it, he's
> gonna throw him off the roof...

> SNOOZE
> Oh shit, oh fuck, oh Jesus...

> ANDY
> Because if you <u>do</u> trust her, there's
> no reason in the world you can't
> keep every cent of that money.

Hadley abruptly jerks Andy to a stop right at the edge. In
fact, Andy's <u>past</u> the edge, beyond his balance, shoetips
scraping the roof. The only thing between him and an ugly drop
to the concrete is Hadley's grip on the front of his shirt.

> HADLEY
> You better start making sense.

> ANDY
> If you want to keep that money, <u>all</u>
> of it, just give it to your wife.
> See, the IRS allows you a one-time-
> only gift to your spouse. It's good
> up to sixty thousand dollars.

> HADLEY
> Naw, that ain't right! Tax <u>free?</u>

> ANDY
> Tax free. IRS can't touch one cent.

The cons are pausing work, stunned by this business discussion.

(CONTINUED)

> HADLEY
> You're the smart banker what shot
> his wife. Why should I believe a
> smart banker like you? So's I can
> wind up in here with you?

> ANDY
> It's perfectly legal. Go ask the
> IRS, they'll say the same thing.
> Actually, I feel silly telling you
> all this. I'm sure you would have
> investigated the matter yourself.

> HADLEY
> Fuckin'-A. I don't need no smart
> wife-killin' banker to show me where
> the bear shit in the buckwheat.

> ANDY
> Of course not. But you will need
> somebody to set up the tax-free
> gift, and that'll cost you. A
> lawyer, for example...

> HADLEY
> Ambulance-chasing, highway-robbing
> cocksuckers!

> ANDY
> ...or come to think of it, I
> suppose I could set it up for you.
> That would save you some money.
> I'll write down the forms you need,
> you can pick them up, and I'll
> prepare them for your signature...
> nearly free of charge.
>   (off Hadley's look)
> I'd only ask three beers apiece for
> my co-workers, if that seems fair.

> TROUT
>   (guffawing)
> Co-workers! Get him! That's rich,
> ain't it? Co-workers...

Hadley freezes him with a look. Andy presses on:

> ANDY
> I think a man working outdoors
> feels more like a man if he can
> have a bottle of suds. That's only
> my opinion.

The convicts stand gaping, all pretense of work gone. They
look like they've been pole-axed. Hadley shoots them a look.

(CONTINUED)

58 CONTINUED   58

                              HADLEY
            What are you jimmies starin' at?
            Back to work, goddamn it!

59   EXT - LICENSE PLATE FACTORY - DAY (1949)   59

     As before, an object is hauled up the side of the building by
     rope -- only this time, it's a cooler of beer and ice.

                              RED (V.O.)
            And that's how it came to pass,
            that on the second-to-last day of
            the job, the convict crew that
            tarred the plate factory roof in
            the spring of '49...

60   EXT - ROOF - SHORTLY LATER (1949)   60

     The cons are taking the sun and drinking beer.

                              RED (V.O.)
            ...wound up sitting in a row at ten
            o'clock in the morning, drinking icy
            cold Black Label beer courtesy of
            the hardest screw that ever walked
            a turn at Shawshank State Prison.

                              HADLEY
            Drink up, boys. While it's cold.

                              RED (V.O.)
            The colossal prick even managed to
            sound magnanimous.

     Red knocks back another sip, enjoying the bitter cold on his
     tongue and the warm sun on face.

                              RED (V.O.)
            We sat and drank with the sun on
            our shoulders, and felt like free
            men. We could'a been tarring the
            roof of one of our own houses. We
            were the Lords of all Creation.

     He glances over to Andy squatting apart from the others.

                              RED (V.O.)
            As for Andy, he spent that break
            hunkered in the shade, a strange
            little smile on his face, watching
            us drink his beer.

                              HEYWOOD
                      (approaches with a beer)
            Here's a cold one, Andy.

                                          (CONTINUED)

60 CONTINUED   60

                              ANDY
                    No thanks. I gave up drinking.

          Heywood drifts back to others, giving them a look.

                              RED (V.O.)
                    You could argue he'd done it to
                    curry favor with the guards. Or
                    maybe make a few friends among us
                    cons. Me, I think he did it just to
                    feel normal again...if only for a
                    short while.

61   EXT - PRISON YARD - THE BLEACHERS - DAY (1949)   61

          Andy and Red play checkers. Red makes his move.

                              RED
                    King me.

                              ANDY
                    Chess. Now there's a game of kings.
                    Civilized...strategic...

                              RED
                    ...and totally fuckin'
                    inexplicable. Hate that game.

                              ANDY
                    Maybe you'll let me teach you
                    someday. I've been thinking of
                    getting a board together.

                              RED
                    You come to the right place. I'm
                    the man who can get things.

                              ANDY
                    We might do business on a board. But
                    the pieces, I'd like to carve those
                    myself. One side done in quartz...
                    the opposing side in limestone.

                              RED
                    That'd take you years.

                              ANDY
                    Years I've got. What I don't have
                    are the rocks. Pickings here in the
                    exercise yard are pretty slim.

                              RED
                    How's that rock-hammer workin' out
                    anyway? Scratch your name on your
                    wall yet?

(CONTINUED)

61 CONTINUED   61

                                    ANDY
                               (smiles)
                    Not yet. I suppose I should.

                                    RED
                    Andy? I guess we're gettin' to be
                    friends, ain't we?

                                    ANDY
                    I suppose we are.

                                    RED
                    I ask a question? Why'd you do it?

                                    ANDY
                    I'm innocent, remember? Just like
                    everybody else here.

Red takes this as a gentle rebuff, keeps playing.

                                    ANDY
                    What are <u>you</u> in for, Red?

                                    RED
                    Murder. Same as you.

                                    ANDY
                    Innocent?

                                    RED
                    The only guilty man in Shawshank.

62   INT - ANDY'S CELL - NIGHT (1949)   62

Andy lies in his bunk after lights out, polishing a fragment
of quartz by the light of the moon. He pauses, glancing at
all the names scratched in the wall. He rises, makes sure
the coast is clear, and starts scratching his name into the
cement with his rock-hammer, adding to the record.

63   RAY MILLAND   63

fills the screen in glorious (and scratchy) black & white,
suffering a bad case of DT's...

64   INT - PRISON AUDITORIUM - NIGHT (1949)   64

...while a CONVICT AUDIENCE hoots and catcalls, talking back
to the screen. We find Red slouched in a folding chair,
watching the movie. Andy enters, backlit by the flickering
glare of the projector, and takes a seat next to him.

                                    RED
                    Here's the good part. Bugs come out
                    of the walls to get his ass.

(CONTINUED)

64 CONTINUED   64

                              ANDY
                    I know. I've seen it three times
                    this month already.

Ray Milland starts SCREAMING. The entire audience SCREAMS with
him, high-pitched and hysterical. Andy fidgets.

                              ANDY
                    Can we talk business?

                              RED
                    Sure. What do you want?

                              ANDY
                    Rita Hayworth. Can you get her?

                              RED
                    No problem. Take a few weeks.

                              ANDY
                    Weeks?

                              RED
                    Don't have her stuffed down my
                    pants this very moment, sorry to
                    say. Relax. What are you so nervous
                    about? She's just a woman.

Andy nods, embarrassed. He gets up and hurries out. Red grins,
turns back to the movie.

65   INT - AUDITORIUM CORRIDOR - NIGHT (1949)   65

Andy exits the theater and freezes in his tracks. Two dark
figures loom in the corridor, blocking his path. Rooster and
Pete. Andy turns back -- and runs right into Bogs. Instant
bear hug. The Sisters are on him like a flash. They kick a
door open and drag him into --

66   THE PROJECTION BOOTH   66

-- where they confront the startled PROJECTIONIST, an old con
blinking at them through thick bifocals.

                              BOGS
                    Take a walk.

                              PROJECTIONIST
                    I have to change reels.

                              BOGS
                    I said fuck off.

Terrified, the old man darts past and out the door. Pete slams
and locks it. Bogs shoves Andy to the center of the room.

(CONTINUED)

                              BOGS
                    Ain't you gonna scream?

Andy sighs, cocks his head at the projector.

                              ANDY
                    They'd never hear me over that.
                    Let's get this over with.

Seemingly resigned, Andy turns around, leans on the rewind
bench -- and curls his fingers around a full 1,000 foot reel
of 35mm film. Rooster licks his lips, pushes past the others.

                              ROOSTER
                    Me first.

                              ANDY
                    Okay.

Andy whips the reel of film around in a vicious arc, smashing
it into Rooster's face and bouncing him off the wall.

                              ROOSTER
                    Fuck! Shit! He broke my nose!

Andy fights like hell, but is soon overpowered and forced to his
knees. Bogs steps to Andy, pulls out an awl with a vicious
eight-inch spike, gives him a good long look at it.

                              BOGS
                    Now I'm gonna open my fly, and
                    you're gonna swallow what I give
                    you to swallow. And when you
                    swallowed mine, you gonna swallow
                    Rooster's. You done broke his nose,
                    so he ought to have somethin' to
                    show for it.

                              ANDY
                    Anything you put in my mouth,
                    you're going to lose.

                              BOGS
                    You don't understand. You do that,
                    I'll put all eight inches of this
                    steel in your ear.

                              ANDY
                    Okay. But you should know that
                    sudden serious brain injury causes
                    the victim to bite down. Hard.
                              (faint smile)
                    In fact, I understand the bite-reflex
                    is so strong the victim's jaws have
                    to be pried open with a crowbar.

66 CONTINUED   66

>   The Sisters consider this carefully. The film runs out of the
>   projector, flapping on the reel. The screen goes white.

                              BOGS
                    You little fuck.

>   Andy gets a bootheel in the face. The Sisters start kicking
>   and beating the living shit out of him with anything they can
>   get their hands on. In the theater, the convicts are CHANTING
>   AND CLAPPING for the movie to come back on.

                              RED (V.O.)
                    Bogs didn't put anything in Andy's
                    mouth, and neither did his friends.
                    What they did do is beat him within
                    an inch of his life...

67   INT - INFIRMARY - DAY (1949)   67

>   Andy lies wrapped in bandages.

                              RED (V.O.)
                    Andy spent a month in traction.

68   INT - SOLITARY CONFINEMENT - DAY (1949)   68

                              RED (V.O.)
                    Bogs spent a week in the hole.

>   Bogs sits on bare concrete. The steel door slides open.

                              GUARD
                    Time's up, Bogs.

69   INT - CELLBLOCK FIVE - 3RD TIER - DUSK (1949)   69

>   Bogs comes up the stairs, smoking a cigarette. Not many
>   cons around; the place is virtually deserted. A VOICE
>   echoes dimly over the P.A. system:

                              VOICE (O.S.)
                    Return to your cellblocks for
                    evening count.

>   Bogs enters his cell. Dark in here. He fumbles for the light
>   cord, yanks it. The sudden light reveals Captain Hadley six
>   inches from his face, waiting for him. Mert steps in behind
>   Bogs, hemming him.

>   Before Bogs can even open his mouth to say "what the fuck,"
>   Hadley rams the tip of his baton brutally into his solar
>   plexus. Bogs doubles over, gagging his wind out.

70 GROUND FLOOR   70

Ernie comes slowly around the corner, rolling a steel mop
cart loaded with supplies.

71 2ND TIER   71

Red is darning a sock in his open cell. He pauses, frowning,
hearing strange THUMPING sounds. What the hell is that?

72 3RD TIER   72

It's Hadley and Mert methodically and brutally pulping Bogs
with their batons, and kicking the shit out of him for good
measure. He feebly tries to ward them off.

73 2ND TIER   73

Puzzled, Red steps from his cell, following the sound. It
dawns on him that it's coming from above. He moves to the
railing and leans out, craning around to look up --

74 RED'S POV   74

-- just as Bogs flips over the railing and comes sailing
directly toward us, eyes bugging out, SCREAMING as he falls.

75 RED (SLOW MOTION)   75

jumps back as Bogs plummets past, missing him by inches, arms
swimming and trying to grab the railing (but missing that
too), SCREAMING aaaaalll the way down --

76 GROUND FLOOR   76

-- and impacting on Ernie's passing mop cart in an enormous
eruption of solvents and cleansers. The cart is squashed flat,
shooting out from under Bogs and skidding across the cellblock
floor like a tiddly wink, kicking up sparks for thirty yards.
Ernie is left gaping in shock at Bogs and all the Bogs-related
wreckage at his feet.

77 2ND TIER   77

Red is stunned. He very tentatively leans out and looks up.
Above him, Hadley and Mert lean on the 3rd tier railing.
Hadley tilts the cap back on his head, shakes his head.

                              MERT
              Damn, Byron. Look'a that.

                              HADLEY
              Poor fella must'a tripped.

A tiny drop of blood drips off the toe of Hadley's shoe and

splashes across Red's upturned cheek. He wipes it off, then
looks down at Bogs. Cons and guards are racing to the scene.

> RED (V.O.)
> Two things never happened again
> after that. The Sisters never laid
> a finger on Andy again...

78   EXT - PRISON YARD/LOADING DOCK - DAY (1949)   78

Bogs, wheelchair-bound and wearing a neck brace, is loaded
onto an ambulance for transport. Behind the fence stand Red
and his friends, watching.

> RED (V.O.)
> ...and Bogs never walked again. They
> transferred him to a minimum security
> hospital upstate. To my knowledge,
> he lived out the rest of his days
> drinking his food through a straw.

> RED
> I'm thinkin' Andy could use a nice
> welcome back when he gets out of
> the infirmary.

> HEYWOOD
> Sounds good to us. Figure we owe
> him for the beer.

> RED
> Man likes to play chess. Let's get
> him some rocks.

79   EXT - FIELD - DAY (1949)   79

A HUNDRED CONS at work. Hoes rise and fall in long waves.
GUARDS patrol on horseback. Heywood turns up a rocky chunk,
quickly shoves it down his pants. He maneuvers to Red and the
others, pulls out the chunk and shows it to them.

> FLOYD
> That ain't quartz. Nor limestone.

> HEYWOOD
> What are you, fuckin' geologist?

> SNOOZE
> He's right, it ain't.

> HEYWOOD
> What the hell is it then?

> RED
> Horse apple.

                              HEYWOOD
          Bullshit.

                               RED
          No, <u>horse</u> shit. Petrified.

Cackling, the men go back to work. Heywood stares at the rock.
He crumbles it in his hands.

                           RED (V.O.)
          Despite a few hitches, the boys
          came through in fine style...

80   INT - PRISON LAUNDRY - BACK ROOM - DAY (1949)   80

A huge detergent box is filled with rocks, hidden in the
shadows behind a boiler furnace.

                           RED (V.O.)
          ...and by the week Andy was due
          back, we had enough rocks saved up
          to keep him busy till Rapture.

ANGLE SHIFTS to Red as he plops a bag of "laundry" on the
floor. Leonard and Bob toss a few more down. Red starts
pulling out contraband, giving them their commissions.

                           RED (V.O.)
          Also got a big shipment in that
          week. Cigarettes, chewing gum,
          shoelaces, playing cards with naked
          ladies on 'em, you name it...
                   (pulls a cardboard tube)
          ...and, of course, the most
          important item.

81   INT - CELLBLOCK FIVE - NIGHT (1949)   81

Andy, limping a bit, returns from the infirmary. Red watches
from his cell as Andy is brought up and locked away.

82   INT - ANDY'S CELL - NIGHT (1949)   82

Andy finds the cardboard tube lying on his bunk.

                           GUARD (O.S.)
          Lights out!

The lights go off. Andy opens the tube and pulls out a large
rolled poster. He lets it uncurl to the floor. A small scrap
of paper flutters out, landing at his feet. The poster is the
famous Rita Hayworth pin-up -- one hand behind her head, eyes
half closed, sulky lips parted. Andy picks up the scrap of
paper. It reads: "No charge. Welcome back." Alone in the dark,
Andy smiles.

83   INT - CELLBLOCK FIVE - MORNING (1949)   83

The BUZZER SOUNDS, the cells SLAM OPEN. Cons step from their cells. Andy catches Red's eye, nods his thanks. As the men shuffle down to breakfast, Red glances into Andy's cell --

84   RED'S POV - DOLLYING PAST   84

-- and sees Rita in her new place of honor on Andy's wall. Sunlight casts a harsh barred shadow across her lovely face.

85   INT - CELLBLOCK FIVE - NIGHT (1949)   85

Ernie is mopping the floor. He glances back and sees Warden Norton approach the cellblock with an entourage of a DOZEN GUARDS. Still mopping, Ernie mutters to the nearest cell:

                         ERNIE
              Heads up. They're tossin' cells.

Word travels fast from cell to cell. Cons scramble to tidy up and hide things. Norton enters, nods to his men. The guards pair off in all directions, making their choices at random.

                         GUARD
              What kind'a contraband you hiding
              in there, boy?

Cells are opened, occupants displaced, items scattered, mattresses overturned. Whatever contraband is found gets tossed out onto the cellblock floor. Mostly harmless stuff.

A GUARD pulls a sharpened screwdriver out of a mattress, shoots a nasty look at the CON responsible.

                         NORTON
              Solitary. A week. Make sure he
              takes his Bible.

                         CON
              Too goddamn dark to read down there.

                         NORTON
              Add another week for blasphemy.

The man is taken away. Norton's gaze goes up.

                         NORTON
              Let's try the second tier.

86   2ND TIER   86

Norton arrives, makes a thin show of picking a cell at random. He motions at Andy on his bunk, reading his Bible. The door is unlocked. Norton enters, trailed by his men. Andy rises.

(CONTINUED)

86 CONTINUED   86

                          ANDY
          Good evening.

Norton gives a curt nod. Hadley and Trout start tossing the
cell in a thorough search. Norton keeps his eyes on Andy,
looking for a wrong glance or nervous blink. He takes the
Bible out of Andy's hand.

                          NORTON
          I'm pleased to see you reading
          this. Any favorite passages?

                          ANDY
          "Watch ye therefore, for ye know not
          when the master of the house cometh."

                          NORTON
                (smiles)
          Luke. Chapter 13, verse 35. I've
          always liked that one.
                (strolls the cell)
          But I prefer: "I am the light of
          the world. He that followeth me
          shall not walk in darkness, but
          shall have the light of life."

                          ANDY
          John. Chapter 8, verse 12.

                          NORTON
          I hear you're good with numbers.
          How nice. A man should have a skill.

                          HADLEY
          You wanna explain this?

Andy glances over. Hadley is holding up a rock blanket, a
polishing cloth roughly the size of an oven mitt.

                          ANDY
          It's called a rock blanket. It's
          for shaping and polishing rocks.
          Little hobby of mine.

Hadley glances at the rocks lining the window sill, turns to
Norton.

                          HADLEY
          Looks pretty clean. Some contraband
          here, nothing to get in a twist over.

Norton nods, strolls to the poster of Rita.

(CONTINUED)

86 CONTINUED   86

                          NORTON
          I can't say I approve of <u>this</u>...
                    (turns to Andy)
          ...but I suppose exceptions can
          always be made.

Norton exits, the guards follow. The cell door is slammed and
locked. Norton pauses, turns back.

                          NORTON
          I almost forgot.

He reaches through the bars and returns the Bible to Andy.

                          NORTON
          I'd hate to deprive you of this.
          Salvation lies within.

Norton and his men walk away.

                          RED (V.O.)
          Tossin' cells was just an excuse.
          Truth is, Norton wanted to size
          Andy up.

87   INT - PRISON LAUNDRY - DAY (1949)   87

Andy is working the line. Hadley enters and confers briefly
with Bob. Bob nods, crosses to Andy, taps him. Andy turns,
removes an earplug. Bob shouts over the machine noise:

                          BOB
          DUFRESNE! YOU'RE OFF THE LINE!

88   INT - WARDEN NORTON'S OFFICE - DAY (1949)   88

Andy is led in. Norton is at his desk doing paperwork. Andy's
eyes go to a framed needle-point sampler on the wall behind
him that reads: "HIS JUDGMENT COMETH AND THAT RIGHT SOON."

                          NORTON
          My wife made that in church group.

                          ANDY
          It's very pretty, sir.

                          NORTON
          You like working in the laundry?

                          ANDY
          No, sir. Not especially.

                          NORTON
          Perhaps we can find something more
          befitting a man of your education.

89   INT - MAIN BUILDING - STORAGE ROOMS - DAY (1949)   89

A series of bleak rooms stacked high with unused filing
cabinets, desks, paint supplies, etc. Andy enters. He hears a
FLUTTER OF WINGS. An adult crow lands on a filing cabinet and
struts back and forth, checking him out. Andy smiles.

                         ANDY
              Hey, Jake. Where's Brooks?

Brooks Hatlen pokes his head out of the back room.

                         BROOKS
              Andy! Thought I heard you out here!

                         ANDY
              I've been reassigned to you.

                         BROOKS
              I know, they told me. Ain't that a
              kick in the ass? Come on in, I'll
              give you the dime tour.

90   INT - SHAWSHANK PRISON LIBRARY - DAY (1949)   90

Brooks leads Andy into the bleakest back room of all. Rough
plank shelves are lined with books. Brooks' private domain.

                         BROOKS
              Here she is, the Shawshank Prison
              Library. Along this side, we got
              the National Geographics. That
              side, the Reader's Digest Condensed
              books. Bottom shelf there, some
              Louis L'Amours and Erle Stanley
              Gardners. Every night I pile the
              cart and make my rounds. I write
              down the names on this clipboard
              here. Well, that's it. Easy, peasy,
              Japanesey. Any questions?

Andy pauses. Something about this doesn't make any sense.

                         ANDY
              Brooks? How long have you been
              librarian?

                         BROOKS
              Since 1912. Yuh, over 37 years.

                         ANDY
              In all that time, have you ever had
              an assistant?

(CONTINUED)

90 CONTINUED   90

                              BROOKS
                    Never needed one. Not much to it,
                    is there?

                              ANDY
                    So why now? Why me?

                              BROOKS
                    I dunno. Be nice to have some
                    comp'ny down here for a change.

                              HADLEY (O.S.)
                    Dufresne!

91   Andy steps back into the outer rooms and finds Hadley with   91
        another GUARD, a huge fellow named DEKINS.

                              HADLEY
                    That's him. That's the one.

        Hadley exits. Dekins approaches Andy ominously. Andy stands
        his ground, waiting for whatever comes next. Finally:

                              DEKINS
                    I'm Dekins. I been, uh, thinkin'
                    'bout maybe settin' up some kinda
                    trust fund for my kids' educations.

        Andy covers his surprise. Glances at Brooks. Brooks smiles.

                              ANDY
                    I see. Well. Why don't we have a
                    seat and talk it over?

                              BROOKS
                    Pull down one'a them desks there.

        Andy and Dekins grab a desk standing on end and tilt it to the
        floor. They find chairs and settle in. Brooks returns with a
        tablet of paper and a pen, slides them before Andy.

                              ANDY
                    What did you have in mind? A weekly
                    draw on your pay?

                              DEKINS
                    Yuh. I figured just stick it in the
                    bank, but Captain Hadley said check
                    with you first.

                              ANDY
                    He was right. You don't want your
                    money in a bank.

(CONTINUED)

                        DEKINS
        I don't?

                        ANDY
        What's that gonna earn you? Two and
        a half, three percent a year? We
        can do a lot better than that.
                (wets his pen)
        So tell me, Mr. Dekins. Where do
        you want to send your kids?
        Harvard? Yale?

92 INT - MESS HALL - DAY (1949)   92

                        FLOYD
        He didn't say that!

                        BROOKS
        God is my witness. And Dekins, he
        just blinks for a second, then
        laughs his ass off. Afterward, he
        actually shook Andy's hand.

                        HEYWOOD
        My ass!

                        BROOKS
        <u>Shook</u> <u>his</u> <u>fuckin'</u> <u>hand.</u> Just about
        shit myself. All Andy needed was a
        suit and tie, a jiggly little hula
        girl on his desk, he would'a been
        <u>Mister</u> Dufresne, if you please.

                        RED
        Makin' yourself some friends, Andy.

                        ANDY
        I wouldn't say "friends." I'm a
        convicted murderer who provides
        sound financial planning. That's a
        wonderful pet to have.

                        RED
        Got you out of the laundry, didn't
        it?

                        ANDY
        Maybe it can do more than that.
                (off their looks)
        How about expanding the library?
        Get some new books in there.

                        HEYWOOD
        How you 'spect to do that, "Mr.
        Dufresne-if-you-please?"

92 CONTINUED   92

                           ANDY
                 Ask the warden for funds.

     LAUGHTER all around. Andy blinks at them.

                           BROOKS
                 Son, I've had six wardens through
                 here during my tenure, and I have
                 learned one great immutable truth
                 of the universe: ain't one of 'em
                 been born whose asshole don't
                 pucker up tight as a snare drum
                 when you ask for funds.

93   INT - MAIN BUILDING HALLWAY - DAY (1949)   93

     DOLLYING Norton and Andy up the hall:

                           NORTON
                 Not a dime. My budget's stretched
                 thin as it is.

                           ANDY
                 I see. Perhaps I could write to the
                 State Senate and request funds
                 directly from them.

                           NORTON
                 Far as them Republican boys in
                 Augusta are concerned, there's only
                 three ways to spend the taxpayer's
                 hard-earned when it come to prisons.
                 More walls. More bars. More guards.

                           ANDY
                 Still, I'd like to try, with your
                 permission. I'll send a letter a
                 week. They can't ignore me forever.

                           NORTON
                 They sure can, but you write your
                 letters if it makes you happy. I'll
                 even mail 'em for you, how's that?

94   INT - ANDY'S CELL - NIGHT (1949)   94

     Andy is on his bunk, writing a letter.

                           RED (V.O.)
                 So Andy started writing a letter a
                 week, just like he said.

95   INT - GUARD DESK/NORTON'S OUTER OFFICE - DAY (1949)   95

     Andy pops his head in. The GUARD shakes his head.

(CONTINUED)

95 CONTINUED   95

                         RED (V.O.)
            And just like Norton said, Andy got
            no answers. But still he kept on.

96   INT - PRISON LIBRARY/ANDY'S OFFICE - DAY (1950)   96

Andy is doing taxes. Mert Entwhistle is seated across from
him. Other off-duty guards are waiting their turn.

                         RED (V.O.)
            The following April, Andy did tax
            returns for half the guards at
            Shawshank.

97   INT - PRISON LIBRARY - ONE YEAR LATER (1951)   97

Tax time again. Even more guards are waiting.

                         RED (V.O.)
            Year after that, he did them all...
            including the warden's.

98   EXT - BASEBALL DIAMOND - DAY (1952)   98

A BATTER in a "Moresby Marauders" baseball uniform WHACKS the
ball high into left field and races for first.

                         RED (V.O.)
            Year after that, they rescheduled
            the start of the intramural season
            to coincide with tax season...

99   INT - PRISON LIBRARY/ANDY'S OFFICE - DAY (1952)   99

The Batter sits across from Andy. The line winds out the door.

                         RED (V.O.)
            The guards on the opposing teams
            all remembered to bring their W-2's.

                         ANDY
            Moresby Prison issued you that gun,
            but you actually had to pay for it?

                         THE BATTER
            Damn right, and the holster too.

                         ANDY
            See, that's all deductible. You get
            to write that off.

                         RED (V.O.)
            Yes sir, Andy was a regular H&R
            Block. In fact, he got so busy at
            tax time, he was allowed a staff.

(CONTINUED)

99 CONTINUED   99

    ANGLE SHIFTS to reveal Red and Brooks doing filing chores.

> ANDY
> Say Red, could you hand me a stack
> of those 1040s?

> RED (V.O.)
> Got me out of the wood shop a month
> out of the year, and that was fine
> by me.

100   INT - GUARD DESK/NORTON'S OUTER OFFICE - DAY (1953)   100

Andy enters and drops a letter on the outgoing stack.

> RED (V.O.)
> And still he kept sending those
> letters...

101   INT - ANDY'S CELL - NIGHT (1953)   101

Dark. Andy's in his bunk, polishing a four-inch length of
quartz. It's a beautifully-crafted chess piece in the shape of
a horse's head, poise and nobility captured in gleaming stone.

He puts the knight on a chess board by his bed, adding it to
four pieces already there: a king, a queen, and two bishops.
He turns to Rita. Moonlight casts bars across her face.

102   EXT - EXERCISE YARD - DAY (1954)   102

Floyd runs into the yard, scared and winded. He finds Andy and
Red on the bleachers.

> FLOYD
> Red? Andy? It's Brooks.

103   INT - PRISON LIBRARY/ANDY'S OFFICE - DAY (1954)   103

Floyd rushes in with Andy and Red at his heels. They find
Jigger and Snooze trying to calm Brooks, who has Heywood in a
chokehold and a knife to his throat. Heywood is terrified.

> JIGGER
> C'mon, Brooksie, why don't you just
> calm the fuck down, okay?

> BROOKS
> Goddamn miserable puke-eatin' sons
> of whores!

He kicks a table over. Tax files explode through the air.

> RED
> What the hell's going on?

(CONTINUED)

                              SNOOZE
                    You tell me, man. One second he was
                    fine, then out came the knife. I
                    better get the guards.

                              RED
                    No. We'll handle this. Ain't that
                    right, Brooks? Just settle down and
                    we'll talk about it, okay?

                              BROOKS
                    Nothing left to talk about! It's all
                    talked out! Nothing left now but to
                    cut his fuckin' <u>throat!</u>

                              RED
                    Why? What's Heywood done to you?

                              BROOKS
                    That's what they want! It's the
                    price I gotta pay!

Andy steps forward, rivets Brooks with a gaze. Softly:

                              ANDY
                    Brooks, you're not going to hurt
                    Heywood, we all know that. Even
                    Heywood knows it, right Heywood?

                              HEYWOOD
                         (nods, terrified)
                    Sure. I know that. Sure.

                              ANDY
                    Why? Ask anyone, they'll tell you.
                    Brooks Hatlen is a reasonable man.

                              RED
                         (cuing nods all around)
                    Yeah, that's right. That's what
                    everybody says.

                              ANDY
                    You're not fooling anybody, so just
                    put the damn knife down and stop
                    scaring the shit out of people.

                              BROOKS
                    But it's the only way they'll let
                    me stay.

Brooks bursts into tears. The storm is over. Heywood staggers
free, gasping for air. Andy takes the knife, passes it to Red.
Brooks dissolves into Andy's arms with great heaving sobs.

> ANDY
> Take it easy. You'll be all right.

> HEYWOOD
> Him? What about me? Crazy old
> fool! Goddamn near slit my throat!

> RED
> You've had worse from shaving.
> What'd you do to set him off?

> HEYWOOD
> Nothin'! Just came in to say
> fare-thee-well.
>   (off their looks)
> Ain't you heard? His parole came
> through!

Red and Andy exchange a surprised look. Andy wants to
understand. Red just motions to let it be for now. He puts his
arm around Brooks, who sobs inconsolably. Softly:

> RED
> Ain't that bad, old hoss. Won't be
> long till you're squiring pretty
> young girls on your arm and telling
> 'em lies.

104   EXT - PRISON YARD BLEACHERS - DUSK (1954)   104

> ANDY
> I just don't understand what
> happened in there, that's all.

> HEYWOOD
> Old man's crazy as a rat in a tin
> shithouse, is what.

> RED
> Heywood, enough. Ain't nothing
> wrong with Brooksie. He's just
> institutionalized, that's all.

> HEYWOOD
> Institutionalized, my ass.

> RED
> Man's been here fifty years. This
> place is all he knows. In here,
> he's an important man, an educated
> man. A librarian. Out there, he's
> nothing but a used-up old con with
> arthritis in both hands. Couldn't
> even get a library card if he
> applied. You see what I'm saying?

104 CONTINUED   104

> FLOYD
> Red, I do believe you're talking
> out of your ass.

> RED
> Believe what you want. These walls
> are funny. First you hate 'em, then
> you get used to 'em. After long
> enough, you get so you depend on
> 'em. That's "institutionalized."

> JIGGER
> Shit. I could never get that way.

> ERNIE
> (softly)
> Say that when you been inside as
> long as Brooks has.

> RED
> Goddamn right. They send you here
> for life, and that's just what they
> take. Part that counts, anyway.

105   EXT - SHAWSHANK PRISON - DAWN (1954)   105

The sun rises over gray stone.

106   INT - ANDY'S CELL - DAWN (1954)   106

ANGLE ON RITA POSTER. Sexy as ever. The rising sun sends
fingers of rosy light creeping across her face.

107   INT - LIBRARY - DAWN (1954)   107

Brooks stands on a chair, poised at the bars of a window,
cradling Jake in his hands.

> BROOKS
> I can't take care of you no more.
> You go on now. You're free.

He tosses Jake through the bars. The crow flaps away.

108   EXT - SHAWSHANK PRISON - MAIN GATE - DAY (1954)   108

TWO SHORT SIREN BLASTS herald the opening of the gate. It
swings hugely open, revealing Brooks standing in his cheap
suit, carrying a cheap bag, wearing a cheap hat.

Brooks walks out, tears streaming down his face. He looks
back. Red, Andy, and others stand at the inner fence, seeing
him off. The massive gate closes, wiping them from view.

109   INT - BUS - DAY (1954)   109

Brooks is riding the bus, clutching the seat before him,
gripped by terror of speed and motion.

                    BROOKS (V.O.)
               Dear Fellas. I can't believe how
               fast things move on the outside.

110   EXT - STREET - PORTLAND, MAINE - DAY (1954)   110

Brooks looks like a kid trying to cross the street without his
parents. People and traffic a blur.

                    BROOKS (V.O.)
               I saw an automobile once when I was
               young. Now they're everywhere.

111   EXT - BREWSTER HOTEL - DAY (1954)   111

Brooks comes trudging up the sidewalk. He glances up as a
prop-driven airliner streaks in low overhead.

                    BROOKS (V.O.)
               The world went and got itself in a
               big damn hurry.

He arrives at the Brewster. It ain't much to look at.

112   INT - BREWSTER HOTEL - DAY (1954)   112

A WOMAN leads Brooks up the stairs toward the top floor. He
has trouble climbing so many stairs.

                    WOMAN
               No music in your room after eight
               p.m. No guests after nine. No
               cooking except on the hotplate...

                    BROOKS (V.O.)
               People even talk faster. And louder.

113   INT - BROOKS' ROOM - DAY (1954)   113

Brooks enters. The room is small, old, dingy. Heavy wooden
beams cross the ceiling. An arched window affords a view of
Congress Street. Traffic noise drifts in. Brooks sets his bag
down. He doesn't quite know what to do. He just stands there,
like a man waiting for a bus.

                    BROOKS (V.O.)
               The parole board got me into this
               halfway house called the Brewster,
               and a job bagging groceries at the
               Foodway...

114   INT - FOODWAY MARKET - DAY (1954)   114

Loud. Jangling with PEOPLE and NOISE. Brooks is bagging
groceries. Registers are humming, kids are shrieking.

>   WOMAN
>   Make sure he double-bags. Last time
>   your man didn't double-bag and the
>   bottom near came out.

>   MANAGER
>   You double-bag like the lady says,
>   understand?

>   BROOKS
>   Yes sir, double-bag, surely will.

>   BROOKS (V.O.)
>   It's hard work. I try to keep up,
>   but my hands hurt most of the time.
>   I don't think the store manager
>   likes me very much.

115   EXT - PARK - DAY (1954)   115

Brooks sits alone on a bench, feeding pigeons.

>   BROOKS (V.O.)
>   Sometimes after work I go to the
>   park and feed the birds. I keep
>   thinking Jake might show up and say
>   hello, but he never does. I hope
>   wherever he is, he's doing okay and
>   making new friends.

116   INT - BROOKS' ROOM - NIGHT (1954)   116

Dark. Traffic outside. Brooks wakes up. Disoriented. Afraid.
Somewhere in the night, a LOUD ARGUMENT is taking place.

>   BROOKS (V.O.)
>   I have trouble sleeping at night.
>   The bed is too big. I have bad
>   dreams, like I'm falling. I wake
>   up scared. Sometimes it takes me a
>   while to remember where I am.

117   INT - FOODWAY - DAY (1954)   117

>   BROOKS (V.O.)
>   Maybe I should get me a gun and rob
>   the Foodway, so they'd send me home.
>   I could shoot the manager while I
>   was at it, sort of like a bonus.

118   INT - BROOKS' ROOM - DAY (1954)   118

Brooks is packing his worldly possessions into the carry bag.
Undershirts, socks, etc.

                    BROOKS (V.O.)
          But I guess I'm too old for that
          sort of nonsense anymore.

119   INT - BROOKS' ROOM - SHORTLY LATER (1954)   119

Brooks is dressed in his suit. He finishes knotting his tie,
puts his hat on his head. The letter lies on the desk, stamped
and ready for mailing. His bag is by the door.

                    BROOKS (V.O.)
          I don't like it here. I'm tired of
          being afraid all the time. I've
          decided not to stay.

He takes one last look around. Only one thing left to do. He
steps to a wooden chair in the center of the room, pulls out a
pocketknife, and glances up at the ceiling beam.

He steps up onto the chair. It wobbles queasily. Now facing
the beam, he carves a message into the wood: "Brooks Hatlen
was here." He smiles with a sort of inner peace.

                    BROOKS (V.O.)
          I doubt they'll kick up any fuss.
          Not for an old crook like me.

120   TIGHT ON CHAIR   120

His weight shifts on the wobbly chair -- and it goes out
from under him. His feet remain where they are, kicking feebly
in mid-air. His hat falls to the floor.

ANGLE WIDENS. Brooks has hanged himself. He swings gently,
facing the open window. Traffic noise floats up from below.

121   EXT - EXERCISE YARD - SHAWSHANK - DAY (1954)   121

Andy reads the letter to Red and the others:

                    ANDY
          P.S. Tell Heywood I'm sorry I put a
          knife to his throat. No hard feelings.

A long silence. Andy folds the letter, puts it away. Softly:

                    RED
          He should'a died in here, goddamn it.

122   INT - PRISON LIBRARY - DAY (1954)   122

      Andy is sorting books on the cart. He replaces a stack on the
      shelf -- and pauses, noticing a line of ants crawling up the
      wood. He glances up. The ants disappear over the top. He pulls
      a chair over and stands on it, peers cautiously over.

                              ANDY
                  Red!

      Red steps in with an armload of files. Andy gingerly reaches
      in, grabs a black feathered wing, and pulls out a dead crow.

                              RED
                          (softly)
                  Is that Jake?

123   INT - WOOD SHOP - DAY (1954)   123

      Red is making something at his bench, sanding and planing.

                              RED (V.O.)
                  It never would have occurred to us,
                  if not for Andy. It was his idea.
                  We all agreed it was the right
                  thing to do...

124   EXT - FIELDS - DAY (1954)   124

      Low hilly terrain all around. A HUNDRED CONS are at work in
      the fields. GUARDS patrol with carbines, keeping a sharp eye.
      We find Andy, Red, and the boys working with picks and
      shovels. They glance over to the pickup truck. Hadley's
      chewing the fat with Mert and Youngblood. A WHISTLE BLOWS.

                              GUARD
                  Water break! Five minutes!

      The work stops. Cons head for the pickup truck, where water is
      dispensed with dipper and pail. Red and the boys look to Andy.
      Andy nods. Now's the time. The group moves off through the
      confusion, using it as cover. They head up the slope of a
      nearby hill and quickly decide on a suitable spot. The
      guards haven't noticed.

      Jigger and Floyd start swinging picks into the soft earth,
      quickly ripping out a hole. Red reaches into his jacket and
      pulls out a beautiful wooden box, carefully stained and
      varnished. He shows it around to nods of approval.

                              ANDY
                  That's real pretty, Red. Nice work.

                              HEYWOOD
                  Shovel man in. Watch the dirt.

(CONTINUED)

124 CONTINUED   124
        Heywood jumps in and starts spading out the hole.

125   BY THE TRUCK   125

        Youngblood glances up and sees the men on the slope.

                        YOUNGBLOOD
                What the fuck.

                        HADLEY
                   (follows his gaze)
                HEY! YOU MEN UP THERE! GET YOUR
                ASSES OFF THAT SLOPE!
                   (works his rifle bolt)
                YOU HAPPY ASSHOLES GONE DEAF? YOU
                GOT FIVE SECONDS 'FORE I SHOOT
                SOMEBODY!

        Suddenly, other cons start breaking away in groups, dozens of
        them heading toward the slope. The guards look around.

                        HADLEY
                What am I, talkin' to myself?

126   ON THE SLOPE   126

        Andy pulls a towel-wrapped bundle from his jacket and unfolds
        it. Jake. Andy lays him in the box, followed by Brook's
        letter. Red places the casket in the hole. A moment of
        silence. Andy gives Red with an encouraging nod.

                        RED
                Lord. Brooks was a sinner. Jake was
                just a crow. Neither was much to
                look at. Both got institutionalized.
                See what you can do for 'em. Amen.

        Muttered "amens" all around. The boys shovel dirt onto the
        small grave and tamp it down.

127   INT - SHAWSHANK CORRIDORS - DAY (1955)   127

        RAPID DOLLY with Hadley. He's striding, pissed-off, a man on a
        mission. He straight-arms a door and emerges onto --

128   EXT - SHAWSHANK PRISON WALL - DAY (1955)   128

        -- the wall overlooking the exercise yard. He leans on the
        railing, scans the yard, sees Andy chatting with Red.

                        HADLEY
                Dufresne! What the fuck did you do?
                   (Andy looks up)
                Your ass, warden's office, now!

128 CONTINUED   128

    Andy shoots a worried look at Red, then heads off.

129   INT - GUARD DESK/WARDEN'S OUTER OFFICE - DAY (1955)   129

Dozens of parcel boxes litter the floor. WILEY, the duty
guard, picks through them. Hadley enters, trailed by Andy.

                ANDY
        What is all this?

              HADLEY
        You tell me, fuck-stick! They're
        addressed to you, every damn one!

Wiley thrusts an envelope at Andy. Andy just stares at it.

              WILEY
        Well, take it.

Andy takes the envelope, pulls out a letter, reads:

              ANDY
        "Dear Mr. Dufresne. In response to
        your repeated inquiries, the State
        Senate has allocated the enclosed
        funds for your library project..."
           (stunned, examines check)
        This is two hundred dollars.

Wiley grins. Hadley glares at him. The grin vanishes.

              ANDY
        "In addition, the Library District
        has generously responded with a
        charitable donation of used books
        and sundries. We trust this will
        fill your needs. We now consider
        the matter closed. Please stop
        sending us letters. Yours truly,
        the State Comptroller's Office."

Andy gazes around at the boxes. The riches of the world lay at
his feet. His eyes mist with emotion at the sight.

              HADLEY
        I want all this cleared out before
        the warden gets back, I shit you not.

Hadley exits. Andy touches the boxes like a love-struck man
touching a beautiful woman. Wiley grins.

              WILEY
        Good for you, Andy.

                      (CONTINUED)

> ANDY
>
> Only took six years.
>   (beat)
> From now on, I send two letters a
> week instead of one.
>
> WILEY
>   (laughs, shakes his head)
> I believe you're crazy enough. You
> better get this stuff downstairs
> like the Captain said. I'm gonna go
> pinch a loaf. When I get back, this
> is all gone, right?

Andy nods. Wiley disappears into the toilet, Jughead Comix in
hand. Alone now, Andy starts going through the boxes like a
starving man exploring packages of food. He doesn't know where
to turn first. He gets giddy, ripping boxes open and pulling
out books, touching them, smelling them.

He rips open another box. This one contains an old phonograph
player, industrial gray and green, the words "Portland Public
School District" stenciled on the side. The box also contains
stacks and stacks of used record albums.

Andy reverently slips a stack from the box and starts flipping
through them. Used Nat King Coles, Bing Crosbys, etc.
He comes across a certain album -- Mozart's "Le Nozze de
Figaro." He pulls it from the stack, gazing upon it as a man
transfixed. It is a thing of beauty. It is the Grail.

130   INT - BATHROOM - DAY (1955)   130

Wiley sits in one of the stalls, Jughead comic on his knees.

131   INT - GUARD STATION/OUTER OFFICE - DAY (1955)   131

Andy wrestles the phonograph player onto the guards' desk,
sweeping things onto the floor in his haste. He plugs the
machine in. A red light warms up. The platter starts spinning.

He slides the Mozart album from its sleeve, lays it on the
platter, and lowers the tone arm to his favorite cut. The
needle HISSES in the groove...and the MUSIC begins, lilting
and gorgeous. Andy sinks into Wiley's chair, overcome by its
beauty. It is "Deutino: Che soave zeffiretto," a duet sung by
Susanna and the Contessa.

132   INT - BATHROOM - DAY (1955)   132

Wiley pauses reading, puzzled. He thinks he hears music.

> WILEY
> Andy? You hear that?

133 INT - GUARD STATION/OUTER OFFICE - DAY (1955)   133

Andy shoots a look at the bathroom...and smiles. Go for broke.
He lunges to his feet and barricades the front door, then the
bathroom. He returns to the desk and positions the P.A.
microphone. He works up his courage, then flicks all the
toggles to "on." A SQUEAL OF FEEDBACK echoes briefly...

134 INT/EXT - VARIOUS P.A. SPEAKERS - DAY (1955)   134

...and the Mozart is suddenly broadcast all over the prison.

135 INT - BATHROOM - DAY (1955)   135

Wiley lunges to his feet, pants tangling around his ankles.

136 INT/EXT - SHAWSHANK PRISON - VARIOUS LOCATIONS - DAY (1955) 136

Cons all over the prison stop whatever they're doing, freezing
in mid-step to listen, gazing up at the speakers.

137 The stamping machines in the plate shop are shut down... 137

138 The laundry line goes silent, grinding to a halt... 138

139 The wood shop machines are turned off, buzzing to a stop... 139

140 The motor pool...the kitchen...the loading dock...the exercise 140
thru yard...the numbing routine of prison life itself...all grinds thru
143 to a stuttering halt. Nobody moves, nobody speaks. Everybody 143
just stands in place, listening to the MUSIC, hypnotized.

144 INT - GUARD STATION - DAY (1955)   144

Andy is reclined in the chair, transported, arms fluidly
conducting the music. Ecstasy and rapture. Shawshank no
longer exists. It has been banished from the mind of men.

145 EXT - EXERCISE YARD - DAY (1955)   145

CAMERA TRACKS along groups of men, all riveted.

                    RED (V.O.)
          I have no idea to this day what
          them two Italian ladies were
          singin' about. Truth is, I don't
          want to know. Some things are best
          left unsaid. I like to think they
          were singin' about something so
          beautiful it can't be expressed in
          words, and makes your heart ache
          because of it.

CAMERA brings us to Red.

(CONTINUED)

145 CONTINUED   145

                            RED (V.O.)
            I tell you, those voices <u>soared</u>.
            Higher and farther than anybody in
            a gray place dares to dream. It was
            like some beautiful bird flapped
            into our drab little cage and made
            these walls dissolve away...and for
            the briefest of moments -- every
            last man at Shawshank felt free.

146 INT - PRISON CORRIDOR - DAY (1955)   146

     FAST DOLLY with Norton striding up the hallway with Hadley.

                            RED (V.O.)
            It pissed the warden off something
            terrible.

147 INT - GUARD STATION/OUTER OFFICE - DAY (1955)   147

     Norton and Hadley break the door in. Andy looks up with a
     sublime smile. We hear Wiley POUNDING on the bathroom door:

                            WILEY (O.S.)
            LET ME OUUUUT!

148 INT - SOLITARY WING - DAY (1955)   148

     LOW ANGLE SLOW PUSH IN on the massive, rust-streaked steel
     door. God, this is a terrible place to be.

                            RED (V.O.)
            Andy got two weeks in the hole for
            that little stunt.

149 INT - SOLITARY CONFINEMENT - DAY (1955)   149

     Andy doesn't seem to mind. His arms sweep to the music still
     playing in his head. We hear a FAINT ECHO of the soaring duet.

150 INT - MESS HALL - DAY (1955)   150

                            HEYWOOD
            Couldn't play somethin' good, huh?
            Hank Williams?

                            ANDY
            They broke the door down before I
            could take requests.

                            FLOYD
            Was it worth two weeks in the hole?

                            ANDY
            Easiest time I ever did.

(CONTINUED)

150 CONTINUED   150

                              HEYWOOD
              Shit. No such thing as easy time in
              the hole. A week seems like a year.

                              ANDY
              I had Mr. Mozart to keep me company.
              Hardly felt the time at all.

                              RED
              Oh, they let you tote that record
              player down there, huh? I could'a
              swore they confiscated that stuff.

                              ANDY
                    (taps his heart, his head)
              The music was here...and here.
              That's the one thing they can't
              confiscate, not ever. That's the
              beauty of it. Haven't you ever felt
              that way about music, Red?

                              RED
              Played a mean harmonica as a younger
              man. Lost my taste for it. Didn't
              make much sense on the inside.

                              ANDY
              Here's where it makes <u>most</u> sense.
              We need it so we don't forget.

                              RED
              Forget?

                              ANDY
              That there are things in this world
              not carved out of gray stone. That
              there's a small place inside of us
              they can never lock away, and that
              place is called hope.

                              RED
              Hope is a dangerous thing. Drive a
              man insane. It's got no place here.
              Better get used to the idea.

                              ANDY
                    (softly)
              Like Brooks did?

                                        FADE TO BLACK

151   AN IRON-BARRED DOOR   151

       slides open with an enormous CLANG. A stark room beyond.
       CAMERA PUSHES through. SEVEN HUMORLESS MEN sit at a long

table. An empty chair faces them. We are again in:

INT - SHAWSHANK HEARINGS ROOM - DAY (1957)

Red enters, ten years older than when we first saw him at a parole hearing. He removes his cap and sits.

> MAN #1
> It says here you've served thirty years of a life sentence.

> MAN #2
> You feel you've been rehabilitated?

> RED
> Yes sir, without a doubt. I can say I'm a changed man. No danger to society, that's the God's honest truth. Absolutely rehabilitated.

CLOSEUP - PAROLE FORM

A big rubber stamp slams down: "REJECTED."

152   EXT - PRISON YARD - DUSK (1957)   152

Red emerges into fading daylight. Andy's waiting for him.

> RED
> Same old, same old. Thirty years. Jesus. When you say it like that...

> ANDY
> You wonder where it went. I wonder where ten years went.

Red nods, solemn. They settle in on the bleachers. Andy pulls a small box from his sweater, hands it to Red.

> ANDY
> Anniversary gift. Open it.

Red does. Inside the box, on a thin layer of cotton, is a shiny new harmonica, bright aluminum and circus-red.

> ANDY
> Had to go through one of your competitors. Hope you don't mind. Wanted it to be a surprise.

> RED
> It's very pretty, Andy. Thank you.

> ANDY
> You gonna play something?

152 CONTINUED   152

> Red considers it, shakes his head. Softly:

                         RED
>   Not today.

153 INT - CELLBLOCK FIVE/ANDY'S CELL - NIGHT (1957)   153

> Men line the tiers as the evening count is completed. The
> convicts step into their cells. The master switch is thrown
> and all the doors slam shut -- <u>KA-THUMP!</u> Andy finds a
> cardboard tube on his bunk. The note reads: "A new girl for
> your 10 year anniversary. From your pal. Red."

154 INT - ANDY'S CELL - LATER (1957)   154

> Marilyn Monroe's face fills the screen. SLOW PULL BACK reveals
> the new poster: the famous shot from "The Seven Year Itch,"
> on the subway grate with skirt billowing up. Andy sits gazing
> at her as lights-out commences...

155 INT - RED'S CELL - NIGHT (1957)   155

> ...and we find Red gazing blankly as darkness takes the
> cellblock. Adding up the months, weeks, days...

> He regards the harmonica like a man confronted with a Martian
> artifact. He considers trying it out -- even holds it briefly
> to his lips, almost embarrassed -- but puts it back in its box
> untested. And there the harmonica will stay...

                              FADE TO BLACK

156 WE HOLD IN BLACKNESS as THUMPING SOUNDS grow louder... 156

                         RED (V.O.)
>   Andy was as good as his word. He
>   kept writing to the State Senate.
>   Two letters a week instead of one.

> ...and the BLACKNESS disintegrates as a wall tumbles before
> our eyes, revealing a WORK CREW with picks and sledgehammers,
> faces obscured outlaw-style with kerchiefs against the dust.
> Behind them are GUARDS overseeing the work.

> Andy yanks his kerchief down, grinning in exhilaration. Red
> and the others follow suit. They step through the hole in the
> wall, exploring what used to be a sealed-off storage room.

                         RED (V.O.)
>   In 1959, the folks up Augusta way
>   finally clued in to the fact they
>   couldn't buy him off with just a
>   200 dollar check. Appropriations
>   Committee voted an annual payment of
>   500 dollars, just to shut him up.

157   INT - PRISON LIBRARY - DAY (1960)   157

TRACKING the construction. Walls have been knocked down. Men
are painting, plastering, hammering. Lots of shelves going up.
Red is head carpenter. We find him discussing plans with Andy.

                         RED (V.O.)
               Those checks came once a year like
               clockwork.

158   INT - PRISON LIBRARY - DAY (1960)   158

Red and the boys are opening boxes, pulling out books.

                         RED (V.O.)
               You'd be amazed how far Andy could
               stretch it. He made deals with book
               clubs, charity groups...he bought
               remaindered books by the pound...

                         HEYWOOD
               Treasure Island. Robert Louis...

                         ANDY
                       (jotting)
               ...Stevenson. Next?

                         RED
               I got here an auto repair manual,
               and a book on soap carving.

                         ANDY
               Trade skills and hobbies, those go
               under educational. Stack right
               behind you.

                         HEYWOOD
               The Count of Monte Crisco...

                         FLOYD
               Cristo, you dumbshit.

                         HEYWOOD
               ...by Alexandree Dumb-ass.

                         ANDY
               Dumas. You boys'll like that one.
               It's about a prison break.

Floyd tries to take the book. Heywood yanks it back. I saw it
first. Red shoots Andy a look.

                         RED
               Maybe that should go under
               educational too.

159   INT - WOOD SHOP - DAY (1961)   159

Red is making a sign, carefully routing letters into a long
plank of wood. It turns out to be --

160   INT - PRISON LIBRARY - DAY (1963)   160

-- the varnished wood sign over the archway: "Brooks Hatlen
Memorial Library." TILT DOWN to reveal the library in all its
completed glory: shelves lined with books, tables and chairs,
even a few potted plants. Heywood is wearing headphones,
listening to Hank Williams on the record player.

                    RED (V.O.)
          By the year Kennedy was shot, Andy
          had transformed a broom closet
          smelling of turpentine into the
          best prison library in New England.

161   EXT - SHAWSHANK PRISON - DAY (1963)   161

FLASHBULBS POP as Norton addresses MEMBERS OF THE PRESS:

                    RED (V.O.)
          That was also the year Warden Norton
          instituted his famous "Inside-Out"
          program. You may remember reading
          about it. It made all the papers
          and got his picture in LIFE magazine.

                    NORTON
          ...a genuine, progressive advance
          in corrections and rehabilitation.
          Our inmates, properly supervised,
          will be put to work outside these
          walls performing all manner of
          public service. Cutting pulpwood,
          repairing bridges and causeways,
          digging storm drains...

ANGLE TO Red and the boys listening from behind the fence.

                    NORTON
          These men can learn the value of an
          honest day's labor while providing
          a valuable service to the community
          -- and at a bare minimum of expense
          to Mr. and Mrs. John Q. Taxpayer!

                    HEYWOOD
          Sounds like road-gangin', you ask me.

                    RED
          Nobody asked you.

162   EXT - HIGHWAY CONSTRUCTION SITE - DAY (1963)   162

A ROAD-GANG is grading a culvert with picks. There's dust and
the smell of sweat in the air. GUARDS patrol with sniper rifles.
A pushy WOMAN REPORTER in an ugly hat bustles up the grade,
trailed by a PHOTOGRAPHER.

                    WOMAN REPORTER
          You there! You men! We're gonna
          take your picture now!

                    HEYWOOD
          Give us a break, lady.

                    WOMAN REPORTER
          Don't you know who I am? I'm from
          LIFE magazine! I was told I'd get
          some co-operation out here! You
          want me to report you to your
          warden? Is that what you want?

                    HEYWOOD
               (sighs)
          No, ma'am.

                    WOMAN REPORTER
          That's more like it! Now I want you
          all in a row with big bright smiles
          on your faces! Grab hold of your
          tools and show 'em to me!

She turns, motioning her photographer up the grade. Heywood
glances around at the other men.

                    HEYWOOD
          You heard the lady.

Heywood unzips his pants, reaches inside. The others do
likewise. The woman turns back and is greeted by the sight of
a dozen men displaying their penises and smiling brightly. Her
legs go wobbly and she sits heavily down on the dirt grade.

                    HEYWOOD
          C'mon! We're showin' our tools and
          grinnin' like fools! Take the damn
          picture!

163   INT - SOLITARY CONFINEMENT - NIGHT (1963)   163

Heywood sits alone in the dark. He sighs.

                    RED (V.O.)
          None of the inmates were invited to
          express their views...

164   EXT - WOODED FIELDS - DAY (1965)   164

A ROAD-GANG is pulling stumps, bogged down in mud.

                    RED (V.O.)
          'Course, Norton failed to mention
          to the press that "bare minimum of
          expense" is a fairly loose term.
          There are a hundred different ways
          to skim off the top. Men,
          materials, you name it. And, oh my
          Lord, how the money rolled in...

Norton strolls into view with NED GRIMES at his heels.

                    NED
          This keeps up, you're gonna put me
          out of business! With this pool of
          slave labor you got, you can
          underbid any contractor in town.

                    NORTON
          Ned, we're providing a valuable
          community service.

                    NED
          That's fine for the papers, but I
          got a family to feed. The State
          don't pay my salary. Sam, we go
          back a long way. I need this new
          highway contract. I don't get it, I
          go under. That's a fact.
                    (hands him a box)
          Now you just have some'a this fine
          pie my missus baked specially for
          you, and you think about that.

Norton opens the box. Alongside the pie is an envelope. He
runs his thumb across the thick stack of cash it contains.

IN THE BACKGROUND, a winch cable SNAPS and whips through the
air, damn near severing a man's leg. He goes down, screaming
in mud and blood, pinned by a fallen tree stump. Men rush over
to help him. Norton barely takes notice.

                    NORTON
          Ned, I wouldn't worry too much over
          this contract. Seems to me I've
          already got my boys committed
          elsewhere. You be sure and thank
          Maisie for this fine pie.

165   INT - NORTON'S OFFICE - NIGHT (1965)   165

ANGLE on Maisie's pie. Several pieces gone.

                          RED (V.O.)
            And behind every shady deal, behind
            every dollar earned...

TILT UP to Andy at the desk, munching thoughtfully as he
totals up figures on an adding machine.

                          RED (V.O.)
            ...there was Andy, keeping the books.

Andy finishes preparing two bank deposits. Norton hovers near
the desk, keeping a watchful eye.

                          ANDY
            Two deposits, Casco Bank and New
            England First. Night drop, like
            always.

Norton pockets the envelopes. Andy crosses to the wall safe
and shoves the ledger and sundry files inside. Norton locks
the safe, swings his wife's framed sampler back into place. He
cocks his thumb at some laundry and two suits in the corner.

                          NORTON
            Get my stuff down t'laundry. Two
            suits for dry-clean and a bag of
            whatnot. Tell 'em if they over-
            starch my shirts again, they're
            gonna hear about it from me.
                    (adjusts his tie)
            How do I look?

                          ANDY
            Very nice.

                          NORTON
            Big charity to-do up Portland
            way. Governor's gonna be there.
                    (indicates pie)
            Want the rest of that? Woman can't
            bake worth shit.

166 INT - PRISON CORRIDOR - NIGHT (1965)   166

Andy trudges down the corridor with Norton's laundry, the pie
box under his arm.

167 INT - LIBRARY - DAY (1965)   167

TILT UP FROM PIE to find Red munching away as he helps Andy
sort books on the shelves.

                          RED
            Got his fingers in a <u>lot</u> of pies,
            from what I hear.

                         ANDY
What you hear isn't half of it.
He's got scams you haven't <u>dreamed</u>
of. Kickbacks on his kickbacks.
There's a river of dirty money
flowing through this place.

                         RED
Money like that can be a problem.
Sooner or later you gotta explain
where it came from.

                         ANDY
That's where I come in. I channel
it, funnel it, filter it...stocks,
securities, tax free municipals...
I send that money out into the big
world. And when it comes back...

                         RED
It's clean as a virgin's whistle?

                         ANDY
Cleaner. By the time Norton retires,
I will have made him a millionaire.

                         RED
Jesus. They ever catch on, he's
gonna wind up wearing a number
himself.

                         ANDY
              (smiles)
I thought you had more faith in me
than that.

                         RED
I'm sure you're good, but all that
paper leaves a trail. Anybody gets
too curious -- FBI, IRS, whatever --
that trail's gonna lead to somebody.

                         ANDY
Sure it will. But not to me, and
certainly not to the warden.

                         RED
Who then?

                         ANDY
Peter Stevens.

                         RED
<u>Who?</u>

167 CONTINUED   167

                         ANDY
          The silent, <u>silent</u> partner. He's
          the guilty one, your Honor. The man
          with the bank accounts. That's
          where the filtering process starts.
          They trace it back, all they're
          gonna find is him.

                         RED
          Yeah, okay, but who the hell is he?

                         ANDY
          A phantom. An apparition. Second
          cousin to Harvey the Rabbit.
                   (off Red's look)
          I conjured him out of thin air. He
          doesn't exist...except on paper.

                         RED
          You can't just make a person up.

                         ANDY
          Sure you can, if you know how the
          system works, and where the cracks
          are. It's amazing what you can
          accomplish by mail. Mr. Stevens has
          a birth certificate, social
          security card, driver's license.
          They ever track those accounts,
          they'll wind up chasing a figment
          of my imagination.

                         RED
          Jesus. Did I say you were good?
          You're Rembrandt.

                         ANDY
          It's funny. On the outside, I was
          an honest man. Straight as an
          arrow. I had to come to prison to
          be a crook.

168   EXT - PRISON YARD - DUSK (1965)   168

                         RED
          Does it ever bother you?

                         ANDY
          I don't run the scams, Red, I just
          process the profits. That's a fine
          line, maybe. But I've also built
          that library, and used it to help a
          dozen guys get their high school
          diplomas. Why do you think the
          warden lets me do all that?

(CONTINUED)

168 CONTINUED   168

> RED
> To keep you happy and doing the
> laundry. Money instead of sheets.

> ANDY
> I work cheap. That's the trade-off.

TWO SIREN BLASTS draw their attention to the main gate. It
swings open, revealing a prison bus waiting outside.

169   INT - PRISON BUS - DUSK (1965)   169

Among those on board is TOMMY WILLIAMS, a damn good-looking
kid in his mid-20's. The bus RUMBLES through the gate.

170   EXT - PRISON YARD - DUSK (1965)   170

The new fish disembark, chained together single-file. The old-
timers holler and shake the fence. A deafening gauntlet.

171   INT - CELLBLOCK EIGHT - NIGHT (1965)   171

Tommy and the others are marched in naked and shivering,
covered with delousing powder, greeted by TAUNTS and JEERS.

172   INT - TOMMY'S CELL - NIGHT (1965)   172

The bars slam with a STEEL CLANG. Tommy and his new CELLMATE
take in their new surroundings.

> TOMMY
> Well. Ain't this for shit?

173   INT - PRISON CORRIDOR - DAY (1965)   173

DOLLYING Tommy as he struts along, combing his ducktail,
cigarette behind his ear. (We definitely need The Coasters or
Del Vikings on the soundtrack here. Maybe Jerry Lee Lewis.)

> RED (V.O.)
> Tommy Williams came to Shawshank in
> 1965 on a two year stretch for B&E.
> Cops caught him sneakin' TV sets
> out the back door of a JC Penney.

174   INT - WOOD SHOP - DAY (1965)   174

A SHRIEKING BUZZSAW slices ten-foot lengths of wood. Red runs
the machine while some other OLD-TIMERS feed the wood.

> RED (V.O.)
> Young punk, Mr. Rock n' Roll, cocky
> as hell...

(CONTINUED)

Tommy is hauling the cut wood off the conveyor and stacking it.
It's a ball-busting job, but the kid's a blur.

>   TOMMY
>   (slapping his gloves)
>   C'mon there, old boys! Movin' like
>   molasses! Makin' me look bad!

The old guys just grin and shake their heads.

>   RED (V.O.)
>   We liked him immediately.

175   INT - MESS HALL - DAY (1965)   175

Tommy regales the old boys with his exploits:

>   TOMMY
>   ...so I'm backin' out the door,
>   right? Had the TV like this...
>   (mimes his grip)
>   Big ol' thing. Couldn't see shit.
>   Suddenly, here's this voice:
>   "Freeze kid! Hands in the air!"
>   Well I just stand there holdin' on
>   to that TV, so the voice says: "You
>   hear what I said, boy?" And I say,
>   "Yes sir, I sure did! But if I drop
>   this fuckin' thing, you got me on
>   destruction of property too!"

The whole table falls about laughing.

176   INT - LIBRARY - DAY (1965)   176

Poker game in progress. Tommy, Andy, Red and the boys.

>   HEYWOOD
>   You did a stretch in Cashman too?

>   TOMMY
>   Yeah. That was an easy ride, let me
>   tell you. Work programs, weekend
>   furloughs. Not like here.

>   SNOOZE
>   Sounds like you done time all over
>   New England.

>   TOMMY
>   Been in and out since I was 13. Name
>   the place, chances are I been there.

(CONTINUED)

                              ANDY
               Perhaps it's time you considered a
               new profession.
                         (the game stalls)
               What I mean is, you don't seem to
               be a very good thief. Maybe you
               should try something else.

                              TOMMY
               What the hell you know about it,
               Capone? What are you in for?

                              ANDY
                         (wry glance to Red)
               Everyone's innocent in here. Don't
               you know that?

The tension breaks. Everyone laughs.

177   INT - VISITOR'S ROOM - DAY (1965)   177

CAMERA TRAVELS the room. Chaotic. CONS are waiting their turn
or talking to visitors through a thick plexi shield.

                              RED (V.O.)
               As it turns out, Tommy had himself
               a young wife and new baby girl...

Tommy's at the end of the row, phone to his ear. Other side of
the glass is BETH, near tears, fussing with a BABY on her lap.

                              BETH
               ...said we can stay with them, but
               Joey's gettin' out of the service
               next month, and they barely got
               enough room as it is. Plus they got
               Poppa workin' double shifts and the
               baby cries half the night. I just
               don't know where we're gonna go...

PUSH IN on Tommy's face as he listens.

                              RED (V.O.)
               Maybe it was the thought of them on
               the streets...or his child growing
               up not knowing her daddy...

178   INT - LIBRARY - DAY (1965)   178

Tommy enters, the strut gone from his step. A little scared.
He finds Andy filing library cards.

                              RED (V.O.)
               Whatever it was, something lit a
               fire under that boy's ass.

                    TOMMY
          I'm thinkin' maybe I should try for
          high school equivalency. Hear you
          helped some fellas with that.

                    ANDY
          I don't waste time on losers, Tommy.

                    TOMMY
               (tight)
          I ain't no goddamn loser.

                    ANDY
          That's a good start. If we do this,
          we do it all the way. One hundred
          percent. Nothing half-assed.

Tommy thinks about it, nods.

                    TOMMY
          Thing is, see...
               (leans in, mutters)
          ...I don't read all that good.

                    ANDY
               (smiles)
          Well. You've come to the right
          place then.

179 INT - LIBRARY - DAY (1965)   179

We find Andy giving an impassioned reading:

                    ANDY
          "...and the lamplight o'er him
          streaming throws his shadow on the
          floor...and my soul from out that
          shadow that lies floating on the
          floor, shall be lifted nevermore!"

Andy slaps the book shut, immensely pleased with himself.

                    TOMMY
          So this raven just sits there and
          won't go away?

                    ANDY
          That's right.

                    TOMMY
               (beat)
          Why don't that fella get hisself a
          12-gauge and dust the fucker?

180   INT - LIBRARY - DAY (1965)   180

Tommy tries to read as Andy looks on:

                    TOMMY
          "The cat sh--The cat shh..."
                 (glances up)
          The cat shat on the welcome mat?

Andy shakes his head. Not exactly.

181   INT - LIBRARY - DAY (1965)   181

Andy chalks the alphabet on a blackboard.

                    RED (V.O.)
          So Andy took Tommy under his wing.
          Started walking him through his
          ABCs...

182   INT - MESS HALL - DAY (1965)   182

TRACK the table to Tommy and Andy. Discussing a book.

                    RED (V.O.)
          Tommy took to it pretty well, too.
          Boy found brains he never knew he
          had.

183   EXT - EXERCISE YARD BLEACHERS - DAY (1965)   183

                    TOMMY
          The cat sh--shh--shimmied up the
          tree and crept st--stel--stealthily
          out on the limb...

184   INT - WOOD SHOP - DAY (1965)   184

Tommy intent on a paperback, mouthing the words. Behind him,
wood is piling up on the conveyor belt.

                    RED (V.O.)
          After a while, you couldn't pry
          those books out of hands.

                    RED
          Ass in gear, son! You're putting us
          behind!

Tommy shoves the book in his back pocket and hurries over.

185   INT - LIBRARY - DAY (1965)   185

Tommy writes a sentence on the blackboard. Andy steps in,
shows him how to reconstruct it.

185 CONTINUED   185

                              RED (V.O.)
                    Before long, Andy started him on
                    his course requirements. He really
                    liked the kid, that was part of it.
                    Gave him a thrill to help a
                    youngster crawl off the shitheap.
                    But that wasn't the only reason...

186 INT - ANDY'S CELL - NIGHT (1966)   186

     TIGHT ANGLE on chessboard. Most of the pieces complete. PAN TO
     Andy lying in his bunk, carefully polishing...

                              RED (V.O.)
                    Prison time is slow time. Sometimes
                    it feels like stop-time. So you do
                    what you can to keep going...

     ...and we keep going past Andy in a SLOW PAN of the cell.
     Sink. Toilet. Books. Outside the window bars, we hear another
     TRAIN passing in the night...

                              RED (V.O.)
                    Some fellas collect stamps. Others
                    build matchstick houses. Andy built
                    a library. Now he needed a new project.
                    Tommy was it. It was the same reason
                    he spent years shaping and polishing
                    those rocks. The same reason he hung
                    his fantasy girlies on the wall...

     ...STILL PANNING, past a chair, a sweater on a hook...and
     finally to the place of honor on the wall...

                              RED (V.O.)
                    In prison, a man'll do most
                    anything to keep his mind occupied.

     ...where the latest poster turns out to be Racquel Welch in a
     fur bikini. Gorgeous. "One Million Years, B.C." SLOW PUSH IN.

                              RED (V.O.)
                    By 1966...right about the time
                    Tommy was getting ready to take his
                    exams...it was lovely Racquel.

187 INT - LIBRARY - DAY (1966)   187

     Tommy's taking the big test. Andy's monitoring the time. Deep
     silence, save for Tommy's pencil-scribbling. A few old-timers
     are browsing the shelves, sneaking looks their way. Tommy
     tries to ignore them. Concentrate.

     Andy clears his throat. Time's up. Tommy puts his pencil down.

(CONTINUED)

                              ANDY
            Well?

                              TOMMY
            Well. It's for shit.
                    (gets up in disgust)
            Wasted a whole fuckin' year of my
            time with this bullshit!

                              ANDY
            May not be as bad as you think.

                              TOMMY
            It's <u>worse!</u> I didn't get a fuckin'
            thing right! Might as well be in
            <u>Chinese!</u>

                              ANDY
            We'll see how the score comes out.

                              TOMMY
            I'll tell you how the goddamn
            score comes out...

Tommy grabs the test, wads it, slam-dunks it into the trash.

                              TOMMY
            Two points! Right there! There's
            your goddamn score!
                    (storms out)
            Goddamn cats crawlin' up trees, 5
            times 5 is 25, fuck this place,
            <u>fuck</u> <u>it</u>!

Tommy is gone. Red and others stare. Andy gets up, pulls the
test from the trash, smoothes it out on the desk.

188 INT - WOOD SHOP - DAY (1966)   188

Rest break. Tommy and Red sipping Cokes.

                              TOMMY
            I feel bad. I let him down.

                              RED
            That's crap, son. He's proud of
            you. Proud as a hen.
                    (off Tommy's look)
            We been friends a long time. I know
            him as good as anybody.

                              TOMMY
            Smart fella, ain't he?

188 CONTINUED   188

                          RED
               Smart as they come. Used to be a
               banker on the outside.

                          TOMMY
               What's he in for anyway?

                          RED
               Murder.

                          TOMMY
               The hell you say.

                          RED
               You wouldn't think, lookin' at him.
               Caught his wife in bed with some
               golf pro. Greased 'em both. C'mon,
               boy, back to work...

SMASH! Red turns back. Tommy's Coke has slipped from his hand
and shattered on the floor. The kid's gone white as a sheet.

                          TOMMY
                     (bare whisper)
               Oh my God...

189   INT - LIBRARY - DAY (1966)   189

Tommy sits before Andy and Red:

                          TOMMY
               'Bout four years ago, I was in
               Thomaston on a 2 to 3 stretch.
               Stole a car. Dumbfuck thing to do.
                     (beat)
               Few months left to go, I get a new
               cellmate in. Elmo Blatch. Big
               twitchy fucker. Crazy eyes. Kind of
               roomie you pray you don't get, know
               what I'm sayin'? 6 to 12 for armed
               burglary. Said he done hundreds of
               jobs. Hard to believe, high-strung
               as he was. Cut a loud fart, he'd go
               three feet in the air. Talked all
               the time, too, that's the other
               thing. Never shut up. Places he'd
               been, jobs he pulled, women he
               fucked. Even people he killed.
               People that gave him shit, that's
               how he put it. One night, like a
               joke, I say: "Yeah? Who'd you
               kill?" So he says...

190   INT - CELL - THOMASTON PRISON - NIGHT (1962)   190

> BLATCH
>
> ...I got me this job one time
> bussin' tables at a country club.
> So I could case all the big rich
> pricks that come in. I pick out
> this guy, go in one night and do
> his place. He wakes up and gives
> me shit. So I killed him. Him and
> the tasty bitch he was with.
> > (starts laughing)
> That's the best part! She's fuckin'
> this prick, see, this golf pro, but
> she's married to some other guy!
> Some hotshot banker. He's the one
> they pinned it on! They got him
> down-Maine somewhere doin' time for
> the crime! Ain't that choice?

He throws his head back and ROARS with laughter.

191   INT - PRISON LIBRARY - DAY (1966)   191

Silence. Tommy has finished his story. Red is stunned...but
Andy looks like he's been smacked with a two by four.

> RED
>
> Andy?

Andy says nothing. Walks stiffly away. Doesn't look back.

192   INT - NORTON'S OFFICE - DAY (1966)   192

> NORTON
>
> Well. I have to say, that's the
> most amazing story I ever heard.
> What amazes me most is you were
> taken in by it.

> ANDY
>
> Sir?

> NORTON
>
> It's obvious this fellow Williams
> is impressed with you. He hears
> your tale of woe and quite
> naturally wants to cheer you up.
> He's young, not terribly bright.
> Not surprising he didn't know what
> a state he'd put you in.

> ANDY
>
> I think he's telling the truth.

(CONTINUED)

NORTON
Let's say for a moment Blatch <u>does</u>
exist. You think he'd just fall to
his knees and cry, "Yes, I did it!
I confess! By all means, please add
a life term to my sentence!"

ANDY
It wouldn't matter. With Tommy's
testimony, I can get a new trial.

NORTON
That's assuming Blatch is even
still there. Chances are excellent
he'd be released by now. Excellent.

ANDY
They'd have his last known address.
Names of relatives...
          (Norton shakes his head)
Well it's a <u>chance,</u> isn't it? How
can you be so obtuse?

NORTON
What? What did you call me?

ANDY
Obtuse! Is it deliberate? The
country club will have his old time
cards! W-2s with his name on them!

NORTON
          (rises)
Dufresne, if you want to indulge
this fantasy, that's your business.
Don't make it mine. This meeting's
over.

ANDY
Look, if it's the squeeze, don't
worry. I'd never say what goes on
in here. I'd be just as indictable
as you for laundering the money!

NORTON
Don't you ever mention money to me
again, you sorry son of a bitch!
Not in this office, not anywhere!
          (slaps intercom)
Get in here! <u>Now!</u>

ANDY
I was just trying to rest your mind
at ease, that's all.

(CONTINUED)

                              NORTON
                        (as GUARDS enter)
                    Solitary! A month!

Andy gets dragged away, kicking and screaming:

                              ANDY
                    What's the <u>matter</u> with you? It's my
                    chance to get out, don't you see
                    that? <u>It's</u> <u>my</u> <u>life!</u> <u>Don't</u> <u>you</u>
                    <u>understand</u> <u>it's</u> <u>my</u> <u>life?</u>

193 EXT - PRISON YARD - DAY (1966)   193

     Mail call. Men crowd around as names are called out. Red and
     the boys are parked on the bleachers.

                              FLOYD
                    A month in the hole. Longest damn
                    stretch I ever heard of.

                              TOMMY
                    It's my fault.

                              RED
                    Like hell. You didn't pull the
                    trigger, and you didn't convict him.

                              HEYWOOD
                    Red? You saying Andy's innocent? I
                    mean for real innocent?
                        (Red nods)
                    Sweet Jesus. How long's he been in
                    here?

                              RED
                    Since '47. Going on nineteen years.

                              MAIL CALLER
                    Thomas Williams!

     Tommy raises his hand. The envelope gets tossed to him. He
     stares at it. Red peers over his shoulder.

                              RED
                    Board of Education.

                              TOMMY
                    The son of a bitch mailed it.

                              RED
                    Looks that way. You gonna open it
                    or stick your thumb up your butt?

                              TOMMY
                Thumb up my butt sounds better.

He gets hemmed in by the older men. Red snatches the letter.

                              TOMMY
                C'mon, just throw it away. Will you
                please? Just throw it away?

Red rips it open, scans the letter. Expressionless.

                              RED
                Well, shit.

194 INT - VISITOR'S ROOM - DAY (1966)   194

Tommy makes his way through the chaos, finds Beth and the baby
waiting behind the thick plexi shield. He sits, doesn't pick
up the phone. Just stares at Beth. She doesn't know what to
make of it.

He presses a piece of paper against the glass. A high school
diploma. Her face lights up, blinking back tears.

195 INT - SOLITARY WING - NIGHT (1966)   195

LOW ANGLE on steel door. Somewhere behind it, unseen, is Andy.
A rat scurries along the wall. FOOTSTEPS approach slowly.

196 INT - SOLITARY - NIGHT (1966)   196

Andy listens in darkness. The FOOTSTEPS pause outside his
door. The slot opens. An ELDERLY GUARD peers in.

                          ELDERLY GUARD
                Kid passed. C-plus average. Thought
                you'd like to know.

The slot closes. The FOOTSTEPS recede. Andy smiles.

197 INT - PRISON CORRIDOR - NIGHT (1966)   197

We find Tommy on evening work detail, mopping the floors with
bucket and pail. Mert Entwhistle comes into view.

                              MERT
                Warden wants to talk.

198 EXT - PRISON - NIGHT (1966)   198

A steel door rattles open. Mert leads Tommy outside to a gate,
unlocks it. Tommy looks around.

                              TOMMY
                Out here?

                                   MERT
                    That's what the man said.

Mert swings the gate open, sends Tommy through, turns and
heads back inside. Tommy proceeds out across a loading-dock
access for the shops and mills. Some vehicles parked. The
place is deserted. He stops, sensing a presence.

                                  TOMMY
               Warden?

Norton steps into the light.

                                  NORTON
                    Tommy, we've got a situation here.
                    I think you can appreciate that.

                                  TOMMY
                    Yes sir, I sure can.

                                  NORTON
                    I tell you, son, this really came
                    along and knocked my wind out. It's
                    got me up nights, that's the truth.

Norton pulls a pack of cigarettes, offers Tommy a smoke. Tommy
takes one. Norton lights both cigarettes, pockets his lighter.

                                  NORTON
                    The right decision. Sometimes it's
                    hard to figure out what that is.
                    You understand?
                         (Tommy nods)
                    Think hard, Tommy. If I'm gonna
                    move on this, there can't be the
                    least little shred of doubt. I have
                    to know if you what you told
                    Dufresne was the truth.

                                  TOMMY
                    Yes sir. Absolutely.

                                  NORTON
                    Would you be willing to swear before
                    a judge and jury...having placed
                    your hand on the Good Book and taken
                    an oath before Almighty God Himself?

                                  TOMMY
                    Just gimme that chance.

                                  NORTON
                    That's what I thought.

(CONTINUED)

198 CONTINUED   198

    Norton drops his cigarette. Crushes it out with the toe of his shoe. Glances up toward the plate shop roof as --

199 HIGH ANGLE FROM PLATE SHOP ROOF (SNIPER POV)   199

    -- a rifle scope pops up into frame, jumping Tommy's image into startling magnification, framed in the crosshairs.

200 THE SNIPER   200

    rapid-fires a carbine -- <u>BLAM!BLAM!BLAM!BLAM!</u> -- his face lit up by the muzzle flashes. Captain Hadley.

201 TOMMY   201

    gets chewed to pieces by the gunfire. He smacks the ground in a twitching, thrashing heap. Eyes wide and staring. Dead. Surprise still stamped on his face. Silence now. Norton turns, strolls into darkness.

202 INT - SOLITARY WING - DAY (1966)   202

    GUARDS approach Andy's cell. The door is unlocked. Andy emerges slowly, blinking painfully at the light.

203 INT/EXT - PRISON - DAY (1966)   203

    Andy is marched along. Convicts stop to stare.

204 INT - NORTON'S OFFICE - DAY (1966)   204

    Andy is led in. The door is closed. Alone with Norton. Softly:

>   NORTON
> Terrible thing. Man that young,
> less than a year to go, trying to
> escape. Broke Captain Hadley's
> heart to shoot him, truly it did.

>   ANDY
> I'm done. It stops right now. Get
> H&R Block to declare your income.

Norton lunges to his feet, eyes sparkling with rage.

>   NORTON
> Nothing stops! NOTHING!
>   (tight)
> Or you will do the hardest time
> there is. No more protection from
> the guards. I'll pull you out of
> that one-bunk Hilton and put you in
>   (MORE)

(CONTINUED)

204 CONTINUED   204

                           NORTON (cont.)
               with the biggest bull queer I can
               find. You'll think you got fucked
               by a train! And the library? Gone!
               Sealed off brick by brick! We'll
               have us a little book-barbecue in
               the yard! They'll see the flames
               for miles! We'll dance around it
               like wild Injuns! Do you understand
               me? Are you catching my drift?

SLOW PUSH IN on Andy's face. Eyes hollow. His beaten
expression says it all...

205   EXT - PRISON YARD - DAY (1966)   205

Red finds Andy sitting in the shadow of the high stone wall,
poking listlessly through the dust for small pebbles. Red
waits for some acknowledgment. Andy doesn't even look up.
Red hunkers down and joins him. Nothing is said for the
longest time. And then, softly:

                           ANDY
               My wife used to say I'm a hard man
               to know. Like a closed book.
               Complained about it all the time.
                    (pause)
               She was beautiful. I loved her. But
               I guess I couldn't show it enough.
                    (softly)
               I killed her, Red.

Andy finally glances to Red, seeking a reaction. Silence.

                           ANDY
               I didn't pull the trigger. But I
               drove her away. That's why she
               died. Because of me, the way I am.

                           RED
               That don't make you a murderer. Bad
               husband, maybe.

Andy smiles faintly in spite of himself. Red gives his
shoulder a squeeze.

                           RED
               Feel bad about it if you want. But
               you didn't pull the trigger.

                           ANDY
               No. I didn't. Someone else did, and
               I wound up here. Bad luck, I guess.

                                                 (CONTINUED)

                              RED
                    Bad luck? Jesus.

                              ANDY
                    It floats around. Has to land on
                    somebody. Say a storm comes
                    through. Some folks sit in their
                    living rooms and enjoy the rain.
                    The house next door gets torn out
                    of the ground and smashed flat. It
                    was my turn, that's all. I was in
                    the path of the tornado.
                              (softly)
                    I just had no idea the storm would
                    go on as long as it has.
                              (glances to him)
                    Think you'll ever get out of here?

                              RED
                    Sure. When I got a long white beard
                    and about three marbles left
                    rolling around upstairs.

                              ANDY
                    Tell you where I'd go. Zihuatanejo.

                              RED
                    Zihuatanejo?

                              ANDY
                    Mexico. Little place right on the
                    Pacific. You know what the Mexicans
                    say about the Pacific? They say it
                    has no memory. That's where I'd
                    like to finish out my life, Red. A
                    warm place with no memory. Open a
                    little hotel right on the beach.
                    Buy some worthless old boat and fix
                    it up like new. Take my guests out
                    charter fishing.
                              (beat)
                    You know, a place like that, I'd
                    need a man who can get things.

Red stares at Andy, laughs.

                              RED
                    Jesus, Andy. I couldn't hack it on
                    the outside. Been in here too long.
                    I'm an institutional man now. Like
                    old Brooks Hatlen was.

                              ANDY
                    You underestimate yourself.

(CONTINUED)

                                RED
          Bullshit. In here I'm the guy who
          can get it for you. Out there, all
          you need are Yellow Pages. I
          wouldn't know where to begin.
                    (derisive snort)
          Pacific Ocean? Hell. Like to scare
          me to death, somethin' that big.

                                ANDY
          Not me. I didn't shoot my wife and
          I didn't shoot her lover, and
          whatever mistakes I made I've paid
          for and then some. That hotel and
          that boat...I don't think it's too
          much to want. To look at the stars
          just after sunset. Touch the sand.
          Wade in the water. Feel free.

                                RED
          Goddamn it, Andy, stop! Don't do
          that to yourself! Talking shitty
          pipedreams! Mexico's down there,
          and you're in here, and that's the
          way it is!

                                ANDY
          You're right. It's down there, and
          I'm in here. I guess it comes down
          to a simple choice, really. Get
          busy living or get busy dying.

Red snaps a look. What the hell does that mean? Andy rises and
walks away. Red lunges to his feet.

                                RED
          Andy?

                                ANDY
                    (turns back)
          Red, if you ever get out of here,
          do me a favor. There's this big
          hayfield up near Buxton. You know
          where Buxton is?

                                RED
                    (nods)
          Lots of hayfields there.

                                ANDY
          One in particular. Got a long rock
          wall with a big oak at the north
          end. Like something out of a Robert
          Frost poem. It's where I asked my
                    (MORE)

> ANDY (cont.)
> wife to marry me. We'd gone for a
> picnic. We made love under that
> tree. I asked and she said yes.
> (beat)
> Promise me, Red. If you ever get
> out, find that spot. In the base of
> that wall you'll find a rock that
> has no earthly business in a Maine
> hayfield. A piece of black volcanic
> glass. You'll find something buried
> under it I want you to have.

> RED
> What? What's buried there?

> ANDY
> You'll just have to pry up that
> rock and see.

Andy turns and walks away.

206   INT - MESS HALL - DAY (1966)   206

> RED
> I tell you, the man was talkin'
> crazy. I'm worried, I truly am.

> SKEET
> We ought to keep an eye on him.

> JIGGER
> That's fine, during the day. But
> at night he's got that cell all to
> himself.

> HEYWOOD
> Oh Lord. Andy come down to the
> loading dock today. Asked me for a
> length of rope. Six foot long.

> SNOOZE
> Shit! You gave it to him?

> HEYWOOD
> Sure I did. I mean why wouldn't I?

> FLOYD
> Christ! Remember Brooks Hatlen?

> HEYWOOD
> How the hell was I s'pose to know?

> JIGGER
> Andy'd never do that. Never.

(CONTINUED)

206 CONTINUED   206

They all look to Red.

                              RED
            Every man's got a breaking point.

207   EXT - PRISON YARD - ANGLE ON P.A. - DUSK (1966)   207

                         VOICE (over P.A.)
            Report to your cellblocks for
            evening count.

BOOM DOWN to Red and the boys. Convicts drift past them.

                            FLOYD
            Where the hell is he?

                           HEYWOOD
            Probably still up in the warden's.

                         TOWER GUARD
                        (via bullhorn)
            YOU MEN! YOU HEAR THAT ANNOUNCEMENT
            OR JUST TOO STUPID TO UNDERSTAND?

                            SKEET
            Christ. What do we do?

                            FLOYD
            Nothing we can do. Not tonight.

                           HEYWOOD
            Let's pull him aside tomorrow, all
            of us. Have a word with him. Ain't
            that right, Red?

                             RED
                        (unconvinced)
            Yeah. Sure. That's right.

208   INT - NORTON'S OFFICE - NIGHT (1966)   208

Andy's working away. Norton pokes his head in.

                           NORTON
            Lickety-split. I wanna get home.

                            ANDY
            Just about done, sir.

We follow Norton to his wife's sampler. He swings it aside,
works the combination dial, opens the wall safe. Andy moves up,
shoves in the black ledger and files. Norton shuts the safe.

                            ANDY
            Three deposits tonight.

                                            (CONTINUED)

208 CONTINUED   208

Andy hands him the envelopes. Norton heads for the door.

                    NORTON
          Get my stuff down t'laundry. And
          shine my shoes. I want 'em lookin'
          like mirrors.
                    (pauses at door)
          Nice havin' you back, Andy. Place
          just wasn't the same without you.

Norton exits. Andy turns to the laundry. He opens the shoebox.
Nice pair of dress shoes inside. He sighs, glances down at the
old ragged pair of work shoes on his own feet.

209 INT - NORTON'S OFFICE - NIGHT (1966)   209

Andy is diligently shining Norton's shoes.

210 INT - PRISON CORRIDOR - NIGHT (1966)   210

Andy trudges down the hallway, laundry slung over his shoulder.

211 INT - CELLBLOCK FIVE - NIGHT (1966)   211

Andy nods to the GUARD. The guard BUZZES him through.

212 INT - RED'S CELL - NIGHT (1966)   212

Red hears Andy coming, moves to the bars. He watches Andy come
up to the second tier and pause before his cell.

                    GUARD (O.S.)
          Open number twelve!

Andy gazes directly at Red. A beat of eye contact. Red shakes
his head. Don't do it. Andy smiles, eerily calm...and enters
his cell. The door closes. KA-THUMP! We hold on Red's face.

213 INT - ANDY'S CELL - NIGHT (1966)   213

Andy is polishing a chess piece.

                    VOICE (O.S.)
          Lights out!

The lights bump off. He finishes polishing, holds up the piece
to admire. A pawn. He sets it down with the others -- and we
realize it's the final piece for the board. A full set.

He gazes up at Racquel and smiles. Pulls a six foot length of
rope from under his pillow. Lets it uncoil to the floor.

214 INT - RED'S CELL - NIGHT (1966)   214

Red sits in the dark, a bundle of nerves, trying to hold

214 CONTINUED   214

himself still. He feels like he might scream or shake to
pieces. The seconds tick by, each an eternity.

                        RED (V.O.)
            I have had some long nights in
            stir. Alone in the dark with
            nothing but your thoughts, time can
            draw out like a blade...

A FLASH OF LIGHTNING outside his window sends harsh barred
shadows jittering across the cell. A storm breaking.

                        RED (V.O.)
            That was the longest night of my
            life...

215 INT - CELLBLOCK FIVE - MORNING (1966)   215

KA-THUMP! The master lock is thrown. The cons emerge from
their cells and the headcount begins. Red looks back to see if
Andy's in line. He's not. Suddenly the count stalls:

                        GUARD
            Man missing on tier two! Cell 12!

The head bull, HAIG, checks his list:

                        HAIG
            Dufresne? Get your ass out here,
            boy! You're holding up the show!
                    (no answer)
            Don't make me come down there now!
            I'll thump your skull for you!

Still no answer. Glaring, Haig stalks down the tier, clipboard
in hand. His men fall in behind.

                        HAIG
            Dufresne, dammit, you're putting me
            behind! You better be sick or dead
            in there, I shit you not!

They arrive at bars. Their faces go slack. Stunned. Softly:

                        HAIG
            Oh my Holy God.

216 REVERSE ANGLE   216

reveals the cell is empty. Everything neat and tidy. Even the
bunk is stowed. They wrench the door open and rush in, tossing
the cell in a panic as if Andy might be lurking under the
Kleenex or the toothpaste. CAMERA ROCKETS IN on Haig as he
spins toward us, bellowing at the top of his lungs:

(CONTINUED)

216 CONTINUED   216

                              HAIG
              WHAT THE FUCK!

217   INT - NORTON'S OFFICE - MORNING (1966)   217

Norton is kicking back with the morning paper. He notices how
dingy his shoes are. He glances at the shoebox on the desk. He
kicks his shoes off, opens the box -- and pulls out Andy's old
grimy work shoes. He stares blankly. What the fuck indeed.

An ALARM STARTS BLARING throughout the prison. He looks up.

218   EXT - PRISON - DAY (1966)   218

Norton and Hadley stride across the grounds, ALARM BLARING.

                            NORTON
                  I want every man on that cellblock
                  questioned! Start with that friend
                  of his!

                            HADLEY
                  Who?

219   INT - CELLBLOCK FIVE - RED'S CELL - DAY (1966)   219

Red watches as Norton storms up with an entourage of guards.

                            NORTON
                  Him.

Red's eyes widen. Guards yank him from his cell.

220   INT - ANDY'S CELL - DAY (1966)   220

Norton steps to the center of the room, working himself up
into a fine rage:

                            NORTON
                  What do you mean "he just wasn't
                  here?" Don't say that to me, Haig!
                  Don't say that to me again!

                            HAIG
                  But sir! He wasn't! He isn't!

                            NORTON
                  I can see that, Haig! You think I'm
                  blind? Is that what you're saying?
                  Am I blind, Haig?

                            HAIG
                  No sir!

Norton grabs the clipboard and thrusts it at Hadley.

(CONTINUED)

220 CONTINUED   220

                              NORTON
              What about you? You blind? Tell me
              what this is!

                              HADLEY
              Last night's count.

                              NORTON
              You see Dufresne's name? I sure do!
              Right there, see? "Dufresne." He
              was in his cell at lights out!
              Stands to reason he'd still be here
              this morning! I want him found! Not
              tomorrow, not after breakfast! Now!

Haig scurries out, gathering men. Norton spins to Red.

                              NORTON
              Well?

                              RED
              Well what?

                              NORTON
              I see you two all the time, you're
              thick as thieves, you are! He
              must'a said something!

                              RED
              No sir, he didn't!

Norton spreads his arms evangelist-style, spins slowly around.

                              NORTON
              Lord! It's a miracle! Man up and
              vanished like a fart in the wind!
              Nothin' left but some damn rocks on
              the windowsill and that cupcake on
              the wall! Let's ask her! Maybe she
              knows! What say there, Fuzzy-
              Britches? Feel like talking? Guess
              not. Why should you be different?

Red exchanges looks with the guards. Even they're nervous.
Norton scoops a handful rocks off the sill. He hurls them at
the wall one at a time, shattering them, punctuating his words:

                              NORTON
              It's a conspiracy! (SMASH) That's
              what this is! (SMASH) It's one big
              damn conspiracy! (SMASH) And
              everyone's in on it! (SMASH)
              Including her!

(CONTINUED)

220 CONTINUED   220

He sends the last rock whizzing right at Racquel.

No smash.

It takes a moment for this to sink in. All eyes go to her. The
rock went through her. There's a small hole in the poster
where her navel used to be.

You could hear a pin drop. Norton reaches up, sinks his finger
into the hole. He keeps pushing...and his entire hand
disappears into the wall.

221   ANGLE FROM BEHIND POSTER   221

as Norton rips the poster from before our eyes. Stunned faces
peer in. CAMERA PULLS SLOWLY BACK...to reveal the long
crumbling tunnel in the wall.

222   INT - ANDY'S CELL - MINUTES LATER (1966)   222

RORY TREMONT, a guard barely out of his teens, tries not to
look nervous as they lash a rope around his chest. He's
getting instructions from six different people at once.

                        RED (V.O.)
             They got this skinny kid named Rory
             Tremont to go in the hole. He wasn't
             much in the brains department, but
             he possessed the one most important
             qualification for the job...
                  (they slap a flashlight
                  in his hands)
             ...he was willing to go.

223   INT - TUNNEL - DAY (1966)   223

Rory squeezes down the tunnel on his belly.

                        RED (V.O.)
             Probably thought he'd win a Bronze
             Star or something.

224   INT - VERTICAL SHAFT - DAY (1966)   224

Dark as midnight. Concrete walls rise on both sides. If you
imagine them as two huge slices of bread, the meat of this
particular sandwich is about three feet of airspace and a dark
tangle of pipes between the cellblocks. Rory's appears, shining
his flashlight down the shaft. Somewhere, a rat SQUEAKS.

                        RED (V.O.)
             It was his third day on the job.

(CONTINUED)

224 CONTINUED   224

> RORY
> Warden? There's a space here
> between the walls 'bout three feet
> across! Smells pretty damn bad!

> NORTON (O.S.)
> I don't care what it smells like!

> HADLEY (O.S.)
> Go on, boy! We got a hold of you!

Looking none too happy about it, Rory squeezes from the tunnel
and dangles into the shaft. He gets lowered, shining his
light, smothered by darkness. Not having a good time.

> RORY
> Hoo-whee! Smell's gettin' worse!

> NORTON (O.S.)
> Never mind, I said! Just keep going!

> RORY
> Smells pretty damn bad, Warden! In
> fact, it smells just like shit.

His feet touch the ground -- or what he assumed was the
ground. It's not. In fact, it's just what it smells like. He
sinks in past his ankles. He slips and sits heavily in it.

> RORY
> Oh God, that's what it is, it's
> shit, oh my God it's shit, pull me
> out 'fore I blow my groceries, oh
> shit it's shit, oh my Gawwwwwwd!

225   INT - ANDY'S CELL - DAY (1966)   225

Red and others listen to violent barfing from below.

> RED (V.O.)
> And then came the unmistakable
> sound of Rory Tremont losing his
> last few meals. The whole cellblock
> heard it. I mean, it echoed.

That's it for Red. He starts laughing. Laughing, hell, he's
bellowing laughter, laughing so hard he has to hold himself,
laughing so hard tears are pouring down his cheeks. The look
of rage on Norton's face makes him laugh all the harder.

226   INT - SOLITARY WING - NIGHT (1966)   226

Abrupt silence. LOW ANGLE on steel door.

(CONTINUED)

226 CONTINUED   226

                              RED (V.O.)
                    I laughed myself right into
                    solitary. Two week stretch.

227 INT - SOLITARY - NIGHT (1966)   227

                              RED
                    It's shit, it's shit, oh my God
                    it's shit...

He starts laughing all over again, fit to split.

                              RED (V.O.)
                    Andy once talked about doing easy
                    time in the hole. Now I knew what
                    he meant.

228 EXT - SHAWSHANK PRISON - WIDE SHOT - DAY (1966)   228

Virgin landscape. Charming rural road. Suddenly, State Police
cruisers rocket up the road with SIRENS AND LIGHTS.

                              RED (V.O.)
                    In 1966, Andy Dufresne escaped from
                    Shawshank Prison.

229 EXT - FIELD - DAY (1966)   229

Shawshank is half a mile distant. WE TRACK ALONG a muddy creek
as STATE TROOPERS and PRISON GUARDS scour the brush. A TROOPER
fishes a prison uniform out of the creek with a long stick.

                              RED (V.O.)
                    All they found of him was a muddy
                    set of prison clothes, a bar of
                    soap, and an old rock-hammer damn
                    near worn down to the nub.

TROOPER #2 pulls the rock-hammer from the weeds. SWISH PAN
to a POLICE PHOTOGRAPHER. His FLASHBULB GLARE produces:

230 A BLACK AND WHITE STILL PHOTO   230

of the hapless cops posing with Andy's reeking uniform and the
worn rock-hammer. PUSH IN on the hammer.

                              RED (V.O.)
                    I remember thinking it would take a
                    man six hundred years to tunnel
                    through the wall with it. Andy did
                    it in less than twenty.

231 INT - ANDY'S CELL - NIGHT (1949)   231

Once again, we see Andy using the rock-hammer to scratch his

(CONTINUED)

231 CONTINUED   231

name into the cement. Suddenly, a palm-sized chunk of cement pops free and hits the floor. He stares down at it.

232   INT - ANDY'S CELL - NIGHT (1949)   232

Andy lies in the dark, studying the chunk of concrete in his hands. Considering the possibilities. Wrestling with hope.

                    RED (V.O.)
          Andy loved geology. I imagine it
          appealed to his meticulous nature.
          An ice age here, a million years of
          mountain-building there, plates of
          bedrock grinding against each other
          over a span of millennia...

233   INT - ANDY'S CELL - NIGHT (1949)   233

Andy stands peering at the small hole left by the fallen chunk. Carefully runs his fingertip over it.

                    RED (V.O.)
          Geology is the study of pressure
          and time. That's all it takes,
          really. Pressure and time.

234   INT - ANDY'S CELL - NIGHT (1951)   234

Rita is now on the wall, hanging down over Andy's back.

                    RED (V.O.)
          That and a big damn poster.

TRACK IN to reveal Andy scraping patiently at the concrete.

                    RED (V.O.)
          Like I said. In prison, a man'll do
          most anything to keep his mind
          occupied.

He hears FOOTSTEPS approaching. He smoothes the poster down and dives into bed. A GUARD strolls by a moment later, shining his flashlight into the cell.

235   EXT - PRISON YARD - DAY (1953)   235

Andy strolls along, whistling softly, hands in both pockets. TILT DOWN to his pantleg. Concrete grit trickles out.

                    RED (V.O.)
          It turns out Andy's favorite hobby
          was totin' his wall out into the
          exercise yard a handful at a time...

236   INT - 2ND TIER - NIGHT (1962)   236

A GUARD strolls the tier, shining his flashlight into the
cells. He pauses at Andy's bars, playing the beam over the
sleeping form huddled under the blankets.

237   REVERSE ANGLE (FROM INSIDE ANDY'S CELL)   237

We see what the guard doesn't: instead of Andy's head under
the blanket, it's a wadded-up pillow. The flashlight plays
across the cell, pinning Marilyn Monroe in a circle of light.

238   ANGLE FROM BEHIND POSTER   238

The light illuminates her face through the paper. WIDEN to
reveal Andy lying in his tunnel, holding his breath. The
light clicks off. The FOOTSTEPS move on. He gets back to work.

                    RED (V.O.)
           While the rest of us slept, Andy
           spent years workin' the nightshift...

239   INT - SHAFT - NIGHT (1965)   239

BOOMING SLOWLY UP the shaft. Rats scurry the pipes. Suddenly, a
piece of concrete the size of a quarter jumps free and plummets
down the shaft as the rock-hammer pushes through. The pick
withdraws, replaced by Andy's peering eye.

240   A SERIES OF DISSOLVES (1965 through 1966)   240

takes us through the widening of the hole. First as big as a
tea cup. Then a saucer. Then a dinner plate.

                    RED (V.O.)
           Probably took him most of a year
           just to get his head through.

Andy finally gets his head through, scraping his ears. He's
got a penlight clenched in his teeth. He peers down into the
shaft. At the very bottom, maybe 20 feet down, a big ceramic
pipe runs the length of the cellblock. Beneath its coat of
grime and dust, the word "SEWER" is stenciled.

241   EXT - LOADING DOCK ACCESS - NIGHT (1966)   241

ANGLE LOOKING STRAIGHT DOWN. Below us, Tommy Williams lies
facedown at Norton's feet. Blood is spreading, fanning out on
the pavement. Norton turns, strolls out of frame.

                    RED (V.O.)
           I guess after Tommy was killed,
           Andy decided he'd been here just
           about long enough.

242   INT - NORTON'S OFFICE - NIGHT (1966)   242

Again we see: Andy working. Norton pokes his head in.

                         NORTON
              Lickety-split. I wanna get home.

                          ANDY
              Just about done, sir.

Norton crosses to the wall safe and works the dial, his back
turned. This time, though, <u>we</u> <u>stay</u> <u>on</u> <u>Andy:</u>

He pulls up his sweater, yanks out a large black book and a
stack of files, lays them on the desk. He then grabs the <u>real</u>
ledger and files, jams them down his pants and smoothes his
sweater down. He picks up the bogus stack, crosses to Norton,
and shoves everything in.

243   INT - HALLWAY - NIGHT (1966)   243

Norton exits his office and strolls off whistling. PUSH IN on
the open door. We see Andy at the guard's desk, pulling
Norton's dress shoes from their box.

                         RED (V.O.)
              Andy did like he was told. Buffed
              those shoes to a high mirror shine.

244   INT - NORTON'S OFFICE - MINUTES LATER (1966)   244

Andy sorts through Norton's three suits. He pauses, checking
the gray pinstripe. Nice.

245   INT - CELLBLOCK FIVE - NIGHT (1966)   245

The guard BUZZES Andy through. Andy walks toward us.

                         RED (V.O.)
              The guard simply didn't notice.
              Neither did I. I mean, seriously,
              how often do you really look at a
              man's shoes?

TILT DOWN as he passes by. Yep, he's wearing Norton's shoes.

246   INT - ANDY'S CELL - NIGHT (1966)   246

The lights go out. Andy places the last chess piece. Gazes up
at Racquel. Smiles. Pulls the rope from under his pillow.
He stands and unbuttons his prison shirt, <u>revealing Norton's</u>
<u>gray</u> <u>pinstripe</u> <u>suit</u> <u>underneath.</u> A FLASH OF LIGHTNING floods the
cell, throwing wild shadows.

247   INT - ANDY'S CELL - NIGHT (1966)   247

The storm rages. Andy, naked, carefully slips Norton's folded
suit into a large industrial Zip-Lock bag. Next to go in are the
shoes, chess pieces (already in a smaller bag), black ledger and
files. Last but not least, a bar of soap wrapped in a towel.

248   INT - TUNNEL - NIGHT (1966)   248

Andy, again wearing prison clothes, inches down the tunnel.

249   INT - SHAFT - NIGHT (1966)   249

Andy squeezes through the hole head-first, emerges to the waist.
He reaches for the opposite wall, manages to snag a steel
conduit with his fingers.

Suddenly, a huge rat darts for his hand. Andy yanks away and
almost plummets head-first down the shaft. He dangles wildly
upside-down for a moment, arms windmilling, then gets his
hands pressed firmly against the opposite wall. The rat
scurries off, pissed.

Andy snags the conduit again. He contorts out of the hole and
dangles into the shaft. We now see the purpose for the rope: the
plastic bag hangs from his ankle with about two feet of slack.

He kicks his legs across the shaft, gets his feet braced. With
his back against one wall and feet against the other, he
starts down the shaft. Sliding dangerously. Using pipes for
handholds. Flinching as rats dart this way and that, scurrying
in the shadows. He drops the last few feet to the bottom.

He approaches the ceramic sewer pipe and kneels before it.
Pulls out the rock-hammer and says a quick silent prayer.
Raises the rock-hammer high and swings it down with all his
might. Once, twice -- third time lucky. An enormous eruption
of sewage cascades into the air as if rocket-propelled, the
Mount St. Helens of shit. Andy is instantly coated black. He
turns away and heaves his guts out. The shit keeps coming.

250   INT - SEWER PIPE - NIGHT (1966)   250

Andy peers down through the hole, playing his penlight around.
The inside diameter is no more than two feet. Tight squeeze.
Coated with crud. It seems to go on for miles.

No turning back. He wriggles into the pipe and starts
crawling, plastic bag dragging behind.

                         RED (V.O.)
               Andy crawled to freedom through
               five hundred yards of shit-smelling
               foulness I can't even imagine. Or
               maybe I just don't want to.

251   EXT - FIELD - NIGHT (1966)   251

Rain is falling in solid sheets. Shawshank is half a mile
distant. BOOM DOWN to reveal the creek...and PUSH IN toward the
mouth of the sewer pipe that feeds into it.

                    RED (V.O.)
          Five hundred yards. The length of
          five football fields. Just shy of
          half a mile.

Fingers appear, thrusting through the heavy-gauge wire mesh
covering the mouth of the pipe. Andy's face looms from the
darkness, peering out at freedom. He wrenches the mesh loose,
pushes himself out, and plunges head-first into the creek. He
comes up sputtering for breath. The water is waist-deep.

He wades upstream, ripping his clothes from his body. He gets
his shirt off, spins it through the air over his head, flings
the shirt away. He raises his arms to the sky, turning slowly,
feeling the rain washing him clean. Exultant. Triumphant. A
FLASH OF LIGHTNING arcs from horizon to horizon.

252   INT - ANDY'S TUNNEL - DAY (1966)   252

Once again, we see stunned faces as CAMERA PULLS BACK.

                    RED (V.O.)
          The next morning, right about the
          time Racquel was spilling her
          little secret...

253   INT - CASCO BANK OF PORTLAND - MORNING (1966)   253

The door opens. Spit-shined shoes enter. DOLLY the shoes to
the counter.

                    RED (V.O.)
          ...a man nobody ever laid eyes on
          before strolled into the Casco Bank
          of Portland. Until that moment, he
          didn't exist -- except on paper.

                    FEMALE TELLER (O.S.)
          May I help you?

TILT UP to Andy. Smiling in Norton's gray pinstripe suit.

                    ANDY
          My name is Peter Stevens. I've come
          to close out some accounts.

254   INT - BANK - SHORTLY LATER (1966)   254

The teller is cutting a cashier's check while the MANAGER

carefully examines Mr. Stevens' various I.D.s.

>   RED (V.O.)
>   He had all the proper I.D. Driver's
>   license, birth certificate, social
>   security card. The signature was a
>   spot-on match.

>   MANAGER
>   I must say I'm sorry to be losing
>   your business. I hope you'll enjoy
>   living abroad.

>   ANDY
>   Thank you. I'm sure I will.

>   TELLER
>   Here's your cashier's check, sir.
>   Will there be anything else?

>   ANDY
>   Please. Would you add this to your
>   outgoing mail?

He hands her a package, stamped and addressed. Gives them a
pleasant smile. Turns and strolls from the bank.

>   RED (V.O.)
>   Mr. Stevens visited nearly a dozen
>   banks in the Portland area that
>   morning. All told, he blew town
>   with better than 370 thousand
>   dollars of Warden Norton's money.
>   Severance pay for nineteen years.

255   INT - OFFICE - DAY (1966)   255

A MAN in shirtsleeves is going through the mail on his desk.
He finds Andy's package, rips it open. Pulls out the black
ledger and files. Scans a cover letter. Holy shit. He dashes
to his door and yanks it open, revealing the words on the
glass: "PORTLAND DAILY BUGLE -- Editor In Chief."

>   MAN
>   Hal! Dave! Get your butts in here!

256   INT - SHAWSHANK PRISON - DAY (1966)   256

Norton walks slowly toward his office. Dazed. The morning
paper in his hand. He goes wordlessly past the DUTY GUARD into
his office. Shuts the door. Lays the paper on his desk.

The headline reads: "CORRUPTION AND MURDER AT SHAWSHANK."
Below that, the sub-headline: "D.A. Has Ledger. Indictments
Expected." Norton looks up as SIRENS SWELL in the distance.

257   EXT - SHAWSHANK PRISON - WIDE SHOT - DAY (1966)   257

For the second time, State Police cruisers go rocketing up the
road with SIRENS AND LIGHTS.

258   INT - NORTON'S OFFICE - DAY (1966)   258

Norton opens his safe and pulls out the "ledger" -- it's
Andy's Bible. The title page is inscribed by hand: "Dear
Warden. You were right. Salvation lay within." Norton flips to
the center of the book -- and finds the pages hollowed out in
the shape of a rock-hammer.

259   EXT - PRISON - DAY (1966)   259

Police cruisers everywhere. A media circus. REPORTERS jostle
for position. A colorless DISTRICT ATTORNEY steps forward into
CLOSEUP, flanked by a contingent of STATE TROOPERS.

                        D.A.
            Byron Hadley?

ANGLE SHIFTS to reveal Captain Hadley. Staring. Waiting.

                        D.A.
            You have the right to remain
            silent. If you give up that
            right, anything you say will be
            used against you in court...

TROOPERS move in, cuffing Hadley's hands behind his back. The
D.A. drones on. FLASHBULBS POP. Hadley says nothing. His face
scrunches up. He begins to cry.

                        RED (V.O.)
            I wasn't there to see it, but I hear
            Byron Hadley was sobbing like a
            little girl when they took him away.

Hadley sobs all the way to the car. The D.A. snaps a gaze up
toward Norton's window, motions his men to follow.

260   INT - NORTON'S OFFICE - DAY (1966)   260

Norton is staring out the window as they approach the
building. He goes to his desk, opens a drawer. Inside lies a
revolver and a box of shells.

                        RED (V.O.)
            Norton had no intention of going
            that quietly.

261   INT - PRISON CORRIDORS - DAY (1966)   261

The D.A. marches along amidst a phalanx of TROOPERS.

262   INT - NORTON'S OFFICE - DAY (1966)   262

Norton sits blankly at his desk, revolver before him. The
doorknob rattles, a VOICE is heard:

                         D.A. (O.S.)
                Samuel Norton? We have a warrant
                for your arrest! Open up!

The POUNDING starts. Norton dumps the box of bullets out on the
desk. He starts sorting them to see which ones he likes.

263   OUTSIDE HIS OFFICE   263

Troopers hustle the hapless duty guard to Norton's door as he
fumbles nervously with a huge key ring.

                         DUTY GUARD
                I'm not sure which one it is...

He starts trying keys in the lock. And as the keys go sliding
in one after another...

264   INT - NORTON'S OFFICE - DAY (1966)   264

...so do the bullets. Norton is riveted to the door. For every
key, he loads another bullet. Methodical and grim. He gets the
final bullet in just as the right key slams home. The door
bursts open. Men muscle in. Somebody SHOUTS. Troopers dive in
all directions as Norton raises the gun --

-- and jams it under his chin. His head snaps back as the wall
goes red. His swivel chair does a slow half-turn and creaks to
a final stop. Troopers rise slowly, gazing in horror.

                         RED (V.O.)
                I like to think the last thing that
                went through his head...other than
                that bullet...was to wonder how the
                hell Andy Dufresne ever got the
                best of him.

PUSH SLOWLY to the wall to reveal Mrs. Norton's framed sampler
trickling blood and brains...and we get our final Bible lesson
for today: "HIS JUDGMENT COMETH AND THAT RIGHT SOON."

265   EXT - PRISON YARD - DAY (1966)   265

Mail call. Red hears his name. They pass him a postcard.

                         RED (V.O.)
                Not long after the warden deprived
                us of his company, I got a postcard
                in the mail. It was blank. But the
                postmark said, "McNary, Texas."

266 INT - LIBRARY - DAY (1966)   266

     Red sits with an atlas, tracing his finger down the page.

                         RED (V.O.)
                    McNary. Right on the border. That's
                    where Andy crossed.
                         (shuts the book)
                    When I picture him heading south in
                    his own car with the top down, it
                    makes me laugh all over again...

267 EXT - MEXICO - HIGHWAY - DAY (1966)   267

     A red convertible rips along with Andy at the wheel, cigar
     jutting from his grin, warm wind fluttering his tie.

                         RED (V.O.)
                    Andy Dufresne, who crawled through
                    a river of shit and came out clean
                    on the other side. Andy Dufresne,
                    headed for the Pacific.

268 INT - MESS HALL - DAY (1966)   268

     Heywood is regaling the table with some anecdote about Andy.

                         RED (V.O.)
                    Those of us who knew him best talk
                    about him often. I swear, the stuff
                    he pulled. It always makes us laugh.

     A wild burst of laughter. PUSH IN on Red. Feeling melancholy.

                         RED (V.O.)
                    Sometimes it makes me sad, though,
                    Andy being gone. I have to remind
                    myself that some birds aren't meant
                    to be caged, that's all. Their
                    feathers are just too bright...

269 EXT - FIELDS - LATE DAY (1966)   269

     Convicts hoe the fields. Guards patrol on horseback.

                         RED (V.O.)
                    ...and when they fly away, the part
                    of you that knows it was a sin to
                    lock them up does rejoice...but still,
                    the place you live is that much more
                    drab and empty that they're gone.

     A DISTANT RUMBLE OF THUNDER. Red pauses, gazes off. Storm
     clouds coming in, backlit by the sun. A light drizzle begins.

(CONTINUED)

269 CONTINUED   269

                          RED (V.O.)
            I guess I just miss my friend.

270   INT - PRISON CELL - NIGHT (1966)   270

Red is sleeping. He wakes with a start.

                          RED (V.O.)
            But there are times I curse him for
            the dreams he left behind...

He senses a presence, looks over his shoulder. There's a Rita
Hayworth poster on his wall. He gets out of bed. Rita just
keeps smiling, inscrutable. As Red watches, a brilliant
round glow builds behind the poster, shining from the
tunnel. The poster rips free, charred to ash in the blink
of an eye as a shaft of holy white light stabs into the
cell. Sunlight. Red staggers back against the glare.

A whirlwind kicks up, whipping everything into the air. The
hole in the wall is like a giant vacuum cleaner -- papers,
book, toiletries, bedding -- if it ain't nailed down, it gets
sucked down the hole toward the light. Red fights it, but the
suction drags him closer and closer...

271   RED'S POV   271

...and CAMERA rockets into the hole, getting sucked down an
endless tunnel at impossible speed, the ROAR of air mixing
with his drawn-out SCREAM, closer and closer to the light...

...and erupting out the other side into total silence and a
beautiful white beach. The Pacific Ocean before us. Enormous.
Mind-blowing. Beautiful beyond description. All we hear now
are the gentle sound of waves.

                          RED (V.O.)
            ...dreams where I am lost in a warm
            place with no memory.

A lone figure stands at water's edge. CAMERA KEEPS MOVING,
coming up behind him and TRACKING AROUND to reveal -- Red.

                          RED (V.O.)
            An ocean so big it strikes me dumb.
            Waves so quiet they strike me deaf.
            Sunshine so bright it strikes me
            blind. It is a place that is blue
            beyond reason. Bluer than can
            possibly exist. Bluer than my mind
            can possibly grasp.

272   AERIAL SHOT   272

Nothing for a million miles but beach, sky, and water. Red is

(CONTINUED)

272 CONTINUED   272

a tiny speck at water's edge. Just another grain of sand.

                          RED (V.O.)
          I am terrified. There is no way home.

273   INT - RED'S CELL - NIGHT (1966)   273

Red wakes from the nightmare. He gets out of bed. Moves to the
barred window of his cell. Peers up at the stars.

                          RED (V.O.)
          Andy. I know you're in that place.
          Look at the stars for me just after
          sunset. Touch the sand...wade in
          the water...and feel free.

                                            FADE TO BLACK

274   AN IRON-BARRED DOOR   274

slides open with an enormous CLANG. A stark room beyond.
CAMERA PUSHES through. SIX MEN AND ONE WOMAN sit at a long
table. An empty chair faces them. We are again in:

INT - SHAWSHANK HEARINGS ROOM - DAY (1967)

Red enters, sits. 20 years older than when we first saw him.

                          MAN #1
          Your file says you've served forty
          years of a life sentence. You feel
          you've been rehabilitated?

Red doesn't answer. Just stares off. Seconds tick by. The
parole board exchanges glances. Somebody clears his throat.

                          MAN #1
          Shall I repeat the question?

                          RED
          I heard you. Rehabilitated. Let's
          see now. You know, come to think of
          it, I have no idea what that means.

                          MAN #2
          Well, it means you're ready to
          rejoin society as a--

                          RED
          I know what you think it means. Me,
          I think it's a made-up word, a poli-
          tician's word. A word so young fellas
          like you can wear a suit and tie and
          have a job. What do you really want
          to know? Am I sorry for what I did?

(CONTINUED)

                                MAN #2
                        Well...are you?

                                RED
                    Not a day goes by I don't feel
                    regret, and not because I'm in here
                    or because you think I should. I
                    look back on myself the way I
                    was...stupid kid who did that
                    terrible crime...wish I could talk
                    sense to him. Tell him how things
                    are. But I can't. That kid's long
                    gone, this old man is all that's
                    left, and I have to live with that.
                            (beat)
                    "Rehabilitated?" That's a bullshit
                    word, so you just go on ahead and
                    stamp that form there, sonny, and
                    stop wasting my damn time. Truth
                    is, I don't give a shit.

The parole board just stares. Red sits drumming his fingers.

CLOSEUP - PAROLE FORM

A big rubber stamp SLAMS down -- and lifts away to reveal the
word "APPROVED" in red ink.

275   EXT - SHAWSHANK PRISON - DAY   275

TWO SHORT SIREN BLASTS herald the opening of the main gate. It
swings hugely open, revealing Red standing in his cheap suit,
carrying a cheap bag, wearing a cheap hat. He walks out, still
looking stunned.

276   INT - BUS - DAY   276

Red rides the bus, clutching the seat before him, gripped by
terror of speed and motion.

277   EXT - BREWSTER HOTEL - LATE AFTERNOON   277

Red arrives at the Brewster, three stories high and even less
to look at than it used to be.

278   INT - BREWSTER - LATE DAY   278

A BLACK WOMAN leads Red up the stairs toward the top floor.

279   INT - RED'S ROOM - LATE DAY   279

Small, old, dingy. An arched window with a view of Congress
Street. Traffic noise floats up. Red enters and pauses,
staring up at the ceiling beam. Carved into the wood are the
words: "Brooks Hatlen was here."

280   INT - FOODWAY MARKET - DAY   280

Loud. Jangling with PEOPLE and NOISE. We find Red bagging
groceries. Registers are humming, kids are shrieking. Red
calls to the STORE MANAGER:

                         RED
              Sir? Restroom break sir?

                       MANAGER
                 (motions him over)
              You don't need to ask me every
              time you go take a piss. Just go.
              Understand?

281   INT - EMPLOYEE RESTROOM - DAY   281

Red steps to the urinal, stares at himself in the wall mirror.

                       RED (V.O.)
              Thirty years I've been asking
              permission to piss. I can't squeeze
              a drop without say-so.

A strange east Indian guitar-whine begins. The Beatles. George
Harrison's "Within You Without You..."

282   EXT - STREET - DAY   282

...which carries through as Red walks. People and traffic. He
keeps looking at the women. An alien species.

                       RED (V.O.)
              Women, too, that's the other thing.
              I forgot they were half the human
              race. There's women everywhere,
              every shape and size. I find myself
              semi-hard most of the time, cursing
              myself for a dirty old man.

TWO YOUNG WOMEN stroll by in cut-offs and t-shirts.

                       RED (V.O.)
              Not a brassiere to be seen, nipples
              poking out at the world. Jeezus,
              pleeze-us. Back in my day, a woman
              out in public like that would have
              been arrested and given a sanity
              hearing.

283   EXT - PARK - DUSK   283

Red finds the park filled with HIPPIES. Hanging out.
Happening. Here's the source of the music: a radio. A HIPPIE
GIRL gyrates to the Beatles, stoned, in her own world.

(CONTINUED)

283 CONTINUED   283

                              RED (V.O.)
                    They're calling this the Summer of
                    Love. Summer of Loonies, you ask me.

284 INT - PAROLE OFFICE - DAY   284

Red sits across from his PAROLE OFFICER. The P.O. is filling
out his report.

                              P.O.
                    You staying out of the bars, Red?

                              RED
                    Yes sir. That I am.

                              P.O.
                    How you doing otherwise? Adjusting
                    okay?

                              RED
                    Things got different out here.

                              P.O.
                    Tell me about it. Young punks
                    protesting the war. You imagine?
                    Even my own kid. Oughtta bust his
                    fuckin' skull.

                              RED
                    Guess the world moved on.

285 INT - FOODWAY - DAY   285

Bagging groceries. CHILDREN underfoot. One points a toy gun at
Red, pumping the trigger. Red focuses on the gun, listening to
it CLICKETY-CLACK. Sparky wheel grinding.

The kids get swept off by MOM. Red starts bagging the next
customer. SLOW PUSH IN on Red. Surrounded by MOTION and NOISE.
Feeling like the eye of a hurricane. People everywhere,
whipping around him like a gale. Strange. Loud. Dizzying. It
gets distorted and weird, slow and thick, pressing in on him
from all sides. The noise level intensifies. The hollering of
children deepens and distends into LOW EERIE HOWLS.

He's in the grip of a major anxiety attack. Tries to shake
himself out of it. Can't. Fumbles the final items into the
bag. Walks away. Trying not to panic. Trying not to run.

He makes his way through the store. Blinking sweat. He bumps
into a lady's cart, mumbles an apology, keeps going. Breaks
into a trot. Down the aisle, cut to the left, through the door
into the back rooms, faster and faster, running now, slamming
through a door marked "Employees Only" into --

286   INT - EMPLOYEE RESTROOM - DAY   286

-- where he slams the door and leans heavily against it,
shutting everything out, breathing heavily. Alone now.

He goes to the sink, splashes his face, tries to calm down.
He can still hear them out there. They won't go away. He
glances around the restroom. Small. Not small enough.

He enters a stall. Locks the door. Puts the toilet lid down
and sits on the john. Better. He can actually reach out and
touch the walls now. They're close. Safe. Almost small enough.
He draws his feet up so he can't be seen if somebody walks in.

He'll just sit here for a while. Until he calms down.

287   EXT - STREET - DUSK   287

Red is walking home.

                         RED (V.O.)
                 There is a harsh truth to face.
                 No way I'm gonna make it on the
                 outside.

He pauses at a pawnshop window. An array of handguns.

                         RED (V.O.)
                 All I do anymore is think of ways
                 to break my parole.

The SHOPKEEPER appears at the glass, locking the door and
flipping the sign: CLOSED.

288   INT - RED'S ROOM - NIGHT   288

Red lies smoking in bed. Unable to sleep.

                         RED (V.O.)
                 Terrible thing, to live in fear.
                 Brooks Hatlen knew it. Knew it all
                 too well. All I want is to be back
                 where things make sense. Where I
                 won't have to be afraid all the time.

He glances up at the ceiling beam. "Brooks Hatlen was here."

                         RED (V.O.)
                 Only one thing stops me. A promise
                 I made to Andy.

289   EXT - COUNTRY ROAD - MORNING   289

A pickup truck rattles up the road trailing dust and pulls to
a stop. Red hops off the back, waves his thanks. The truck

                                          (CONTINUED)

289 CONTINUED   289

    drives on. Red starts walking. PAN TO a roadside sign: BUXTON.

290   EXT - MAINE COUNTRYSIDE - DAY   290

    High white clouds in a blazing blue sky. The trees fiery with
    autumn color. Red walks the fields and back-roads, cheap
    compass in hand. Looking for a certain hayfield.

291   EXT - COUNTRYSIDE - DAY   291

    Walking. Searching. The day turning late. Red finds himself
    staring at a distant field. There's a long rock wall, like
    something out of a Robert Frost poem. Big oak tree. Red checks
    his compass. North end. He crosses a dirt road into the field.

292   EXT - HAYFIELD - DAY   292

    Red walks the long rock wall, nearing the tree. A squirrel
    scolds him from a low branch, scurries up higher. Red studies
    the base of the wall. Nothing unusual here. Just a bunch of
    rocks set in stone. He sighs. Fool's errand. Turns to go.

    Something catches his eye. He walks back, squats, peering
    closer. Wets a fingertip and rubs a stone. A layer of dust comes
    off. Volcanic glass. Gleaming black. He tries to get the rock
    out, anticipation growing. It won't come; it's too smooth. He
    pulls a pocketknife and levers the rock free. It tumbles at his
    feet, leaving a ragged hole.

    Red leans down and solves the mystery at last, staring at the
    object buried under the rock. Stunned. It's an envelope wrapped
    in plastic. Written on it is a single word: "Red."

    Red pulls the envelope out and rises. He just stares at it for
    a while, almost afraid to open it. But open it he does. Inside
    is a smaller envelope and a letter. Red begins to read:

                      ANDY (V.O.)
            Dear Red. If you're reading this,
            you've gotten out. And if you've
            come this far, maybe you're willing
            to come a little further. You
            remember the name of the town,
            don't you? I could use a good man
            to help me get my project on
            wheels. I'll keep an eye out for
            you and the chessboard ready.
                (beat)
            Remember, Red. Hope is a good
            thing, maybe the best of things,
            and no good thing ever dies. I will
            be hoping that this letter finds
            you, and finds you well. Your
            friend. Andy.

(CONTINUED)

292 CONTINUED   292

By now, tears are spilling silently down Red's cheeks. He
opens the other envelope and fans out a stack of new fifty-
dollar bills. Twenty of them. A thousand dollars.

293   INT - RED'S ROOM - DAY (1967)   293

Red is dressed in his suit. He finishes knotting his tie, puts
his hat on. His bag is by the door. He takes one last look
around. Only one thing left to do. He pulls a wooden chair to
the center of the room and gazes up at the ceiling beam.

                         RED (V.O.)
                Get busy living or get busy dying.
                That is goddamn right.

He steps up on the chair. It wobbles under his weight.

294   INT - BREWSTER - RED'S DOOR - DAY (1967)   294

The door opens. Red exits with his bag and heads down the
stairs, leaving the door open. CAMERA PUSHES through, BOOMING
UP to the ceiling beam which reads: "Brooks Hatlen was here."

A new message has been carved alongside the old: "So was Red."

295   INT - GREYHOUND BUS STATION - DAY (1967)   295

TRACKING SHOT reveals a long line of people at the counter.

                         RED (V.O.)
                For the second time in my life, I
                am guilty of committing a crime.

CAMERA brings us to Red, next in line, bag by his feet.

                         RED (V.O.)
                Parole violation. I doubt they'll
                toss up any roadblocks for that.
                Not for an old crook like me.

                         RED
                      (steps up)
                McNary, Texas?

296   EXT - TRAVELING SHOT - DAY (1967)   296

A gorgeous New England landscape whizzes by, fields and trees
a blur of motion. ANGLE SHIFTS to reveal a Greyhound Sceni-
Cruiser barreling up the road, pulling abreast of us. CAMERA
TRAVELS from window to window, passing faces. We finally come
to Red gazing out at the passing landscape.

(CONTINUED)

296 CONTINUED   296

                        RED (V.O.)
              I find I am so excited I can barely
              sit still or hold a thought in my
              head. I think it is the excitement
              only a free man can feel, a free
              man at the start of a long journey
              whose conclusion is uncertain...

297 THE BUS   297

     ROARS past camera, dwindling to a mere speck on the horizon.

                        RED (V.O.)
              I hope I can make it across the
              border. I hope to see my friend
              and shake his hand. I hope the
              Pacific is as blue as it has been
              in my dreams.
                        (beat)
              I hope.

298 EXT - BEACH - WIDE PANORAMIC SHOT - DAY (1967)   298

     A distant boat lies on its side in the sand like an old wreck
     that's been left to rot in the sun. There's someone out there.

299 CLOSER ON BOAT   299

     A MAN is meticulously stripping the old paint and varnish by
     hand, face hidden with goggles and kerchief mask.

     Red appears b.g., a distant figure walking out across the
     sand, wearing his cheap suit and carrying his cheap bag.

     The man on the boat pauses. Turns slowly around. Red arrives
     with a smile as wide as the horizon. The other man raises his
     goggles and pulls down his mask. Andy, of course.

                        ANDY
              You look like a man who knows how
              to get things.

                        RED
              I'm known to locate certain things
              from time to time.

     Red shrugs off his jacket and picks up a sander. Together,
     they start sanding the hull as we

                                        FADE OUT

                        THE END

STILLS

Top: *Tim Robbins listens to Mozart and dreams of freedom as Andy Dufresne, a mild-mannered banker falsely convicted of murder.*

Bottom: *Morgan Freeman received his third Academy Award nomination (his first as Best Actor) for his portrayal of Red, a lifer who befriends Andy.*

Previous page: *Searching for rocks in the work field.*

The Bad Guys, clockwise from top left:
1) Bob Gunton portrays the sanctimonious and corrupt Warden Norton. **2)** Clancy Brown as the brutal Captain Hadley. **3)** Bill Bolender as Elmo Blatch, the killer in the shadows. **4)** Mark Rolston as Bogs Diamond, the prison rapist.

The Good Guys, clockwise from top left:
l) Veteran actor James Whitmore delivers a memorable performance as Brooks Hatlen, the elderly prison librarian. 2) William Sadler portrays the Hank Williams-loving Heywood. 3) Brian Libby as Floyd. 4) Gil Bellows in his first film role as Tommy.

The Good Guys, clockwise from top left:
*1) Neil Giuntoli as Jigger. 2) Larry Brandenburg as Skeet. 3) Joe Ragno as Ernie. 4) David Proval as
Snooze.*

Opposite page: *Lining up a crane shot on Terence Marsh's remarkable cellblock set.*
Top: *Red and his gang check out the new fish. From left to right are David Proval, Brian Libby, Joe Ragno, Morgan Freeman, Larry Brandenburg, William Sadler, and Neil Giuntoli.*
Bottom: *Beers on the roof.*

Top: *Filming in the prison mess hall.*
Bottom: *Tommy (Gil Bellows) attends a study session in the library with his mentor Andy (Tim Robbins).*

Top: *Cinematographer Roger Deakins was nominated for an Academy Award and won the American Society of Cinematographers Award for his superb photography of* The Shawshank Redemption.

Bottom left: *Tim Robbins and Frank Darabont between takes during the filming of Andy's arrival at Shawshank.*

Bottom right: *Darabont huddles in discussion with Morgan Freeman in the prison yard.*

Top: *Stuntman Tom Morga (holding stick) leads a fearless posse of Ohio extras that includes real prison guards and local police officers.*

Bottom: *It takes patience to be an extra—just ask the fine men of Mansfield and surrounding areas, seen here waiting for the cameras to roll.*

Top: *Frank Darabont directs Morgan Freeman and Tim Robbins in the prison yard.*
Bottom: *Morning count on Cellblock Five—another view of Terence Marsh's amazing set. Morgan Freeman can be glimpsed at upper right, second from last.*

Top: *Filming on the roof. Note the safety cables anchoring actors Clancy Brown and Tim Robbins.*
Bottom: *Freeman and Darabont between takes in the grocery store.*
Opposite page: *Darabont and producer Niki Marvin at the courtroom location in Upper Sandusky.*
Following page: *William Sadler gets ready to croon those good old* Lovesick Blues *in the Brooks Hatlen Memorial Library.*

MUTATIS MUTANDIS

OR WHY'D SOME STUFF GET CHANGED?
by Frank Darabont

Judging from lectures I've done, the thing that seems to fascinate film students and movie buffs the most is how and why things change along the path from script to screen. Why are some scenes in the screenplay but not the movie? Why did the dialogue change? Why did a given scene shift to a different location?

The answers are as numerous and varied as the films that are made, the people involved, or the shots that comprise a given movie. (We won't discuss the grim specter of studio interference, which is not a factor at Castle Rock.) Some changes are due to the creative input of others. We've all heard the old axiom that film-making is a collaborative process. Actors, producers, production designers, editors, cinematographers, script supervisors—*anyone* who works on a film can have an influence, small or significant, on the final outcome. It usually starts with someone turning to the director and saying, "Hey, what if we tried it *this* way?"

Other changes are rooted in the mundane and sometimes painful fact that—no matter how diligently you try to plan your shoot in preproduction—filming itself is defined by the unexpected. It's a day-to-day (sometimes moment-to-moment) process of being blindsided by the curveballs that God or a random universe decides to throw at you. It's Murphy's Law in its purest form, strolling vengefully hand-in-hand with the fundamental and never-to-be-taken-lightly reality that shooting a movie is a sweaty, desperate game of Beat the Clock. Every creative ambition you have for the film is weighed against the constant ticking, and compromises must inevitably be made. (Robert Benton, a filmmaker I admire enormously, says that every day of shooting feels like a failure for that very reason. I know how he feels.)

Finally there looms the editing room, where the movie is *really* made (everything else is mere preamble). It's where the editor and director write the final draft of the script, using film instead of paper. It never ceases to amaze me how a movie takes on a life of its own during cutting, making its own suggestions and demands. Things that played beautifully on the page can suddenly stick out like a sore thumb. Entire scenes can drop dead altogether.

In short, that path from script to screen can be a twisty and unpredictable one, subject to countless random factors that affect the original creative vision. Needless to say, this can have a somewhat unnerving effect on a director, as he/she has been thinking about the movie for a while (months or years in some cases) and has often developed his/her own preconceptions about the way things should go (compound this unease if said director also happens to be the screenwriter, whose instinct toward guarding the written material is roughly equivalent to that of a badger defending her young). But wimpy preconceptions be damned; God or that cold, uncaring universe will fight you every inch of the way and leave you feeling like Lillian Gish trying to lurch across the shifting ice floes to safety before the waterfall sucks her over the edge.

Sounds pretty dire, but it's just the nature of filmmaking. You either love it or you don't. And the truth is, for every nasty surprise you encounter, a pleasant one pops up to balance things off.

In my six years working on film crews as a set dresser (an invaluable experience I refer to as my "film school"), and my subsequent nine years as a screenwriter, I've been blessed with the opportunity to observe a great many filmmakers plying their trade. It's always struck me that the good ones—the ones I admire most and aspire to be like—seem to realize that a film production is an organic entity, subject not only to vagaries undreamed of, but also to growth. They're adept at thinking on their feet, accommodating the unexpected, turning problems into advantages. They're able to strike a fine balance between being flexible and staying the course, of knowing when to let go and when to force the universe (or cajole the actors) into seeing things their way. Most of all, they're willing to *listen* to the ideas and opinions of others and weigh the value of that input...because the bottom line is, whether it arrives by design or by accident, you never know where a good idea is going to come from. Basically, when all is said and done, luck has a lot to do with it.

In reading the strictly informal, decidedly unscientific mixture of loose analysis and reminiscence which follows, you can decide for yourselves how lucky my colleagues and I were in making *The Shawshank Redemption*. Since the observations it contains are drawn from and inspired by the Q&A sessions I've done at various colleges or other institutes of learning, I'd like to thank the students of the following schools for providing grist for my mill: American Film Institute, CSU Northridge, The Learning Annex, Loyola Marymount, NYU, San Francisco State, UC Berkeley, UCLA, Universidad de Navarra, and USC. May this section provide them further insight (or, at the very least, an occasional chuckle). Mutatis mutandis, y'all.

SCENE BY SCENE

For those who might be unfamiliar with the practice of "scene numbering," I should point out that the small numbers you may have noticed typed into the left and right margins of the screenplay at the heads of scenes are added during pre-production for the mechanical purpose of identifying a given scene during all phases of production. *Everyone* uses them, from the assistant directors scheduling the shoot, to the transportation captain who needs to know where the trucks go and how many picture vehicles appear in any given scene, to the costumers clothing all the actors and extras, to the script supervisor keeping a precise record of shots filmed during each day, to the editor and editor's assistants trying to make sense of all the footage. In short, on any production document or in any discussion, a scene is always referred to by its number—which spares guys like me the embarrassment of turning to the crew and saying, "Uh, you know the scene in the mess hall where they talk about hope...?" Instead, I can come off sounding really professional by referring to it as Scene 150. The same thing applies here:

Scenes 1 through 8. Here's a good example of things reading fine on the page, but not working out quite the same on screen. The screenplay's approach of playing Scenes 1 through 4 (the night of the murder) and Scenes 5 through 8 (the trial) as separate blocks of consecutive narrative proved somewhat protracted and boring when viewed on film. Additionally, the written technique of dividing up Scenes 5 through 8 with "fade to blacks" to accommodate the titles seemed like a good idea at the time, but also served to needlessly protract the sequence—indeed, it managed to stop the narrative flow dead in its tracks.

Preceding and underscoring those problems was the fact that the schedule had allowed only one night to shoot Scenes 1 through 4, including *all* the footage of the lovers as well as Andy in the parked car. It was simply not enough time to shoot everything that was scripted—that clock is always ticking, and summer nights on location in Ohio are incredibly short—so we concentrated on getting all of Andy's footage, which made great sense but left us painfully short on footage of the lovers.

The solution I came up with in the cutting room, heartily embraced by my editor and producer, was to reconceptualize the two separate blocks of narrative into a single title sequence focusing on the trial (really the point of the whole thing), with the footage of the lovers used in a more sparing "flashback" manner. This allowed us to solve two major problems at once: 1) the pacing improved dramatically by getting into the trial in a quicker and more focused way; 2) it spared us the effort (and Castle Rock the expense) of going back and reshooting additional (now superfluous) footage of the lovers. By making do with what we had and rethinking our approach, I believe we improved the sequence (which just goes to show that, sometimes, you *can* fix it in the editing room).

Once the new structure of the sequence was established, we went on what I like to call a "dialogue hunt" (picture Elmer Fudd tiptoeing ever-so-carefully through the forest…), which is where one tries to weed out as many stray lines of dialogue as possible (or stray shots, for that matter) without harming the scene. Most of the dialogue that hit the floor in this instance was spoken by Jeff DeMunn, a superb actor who graced our film with his cameo as the District Attorney (and was gracious enough not to hold his excised lines against me). Scene 7, a swell tracking shot in the jury room, was dropped altogether to further tighten the sequence. The titles themselves were presented in the more traditional manner of playing them over the images, proving once again that some things are traditional because they work.

A quick bit of trivia: when we're with Andy in his car the night of the murder (Scene 3 in the script), the hands that load the gun belong not to Tim Robbins, but to me. This hand-doubling "insert shot," along with three other inserts, was filmed during postproduction on a small stage just a stone's throw from our cutting room at Warner Hollywood Studios. Those four shots represent the sum total of our additional filming once principal photography was completed.

Scene 9. The thing about this scene that inevitably leads people to ask me if Morgan Freeman ever actually *did* go to jail are the very convincing mug shots of what appear to be a young Morgan Freeman attached to the parole form. The answer is no, Morgan never spent any time behind bars. The photos you see are actually of Morgan's son *Alfonso* Freeman, a wonderful young actor who—sans glasses and goatee—is the spittin' image of his old man. These "mug shots" were taken during preproduction by our unit still photographer, Michael Weinstein, whose excellent work is on display in this book. Alfonso also did a wonderful cameo for us as the maniacally laughing con taunting Fat-Ass and the other new arrivals with: "Fresh fish! Fresh fish *today*! We're reeling 'em in!" (Scene 10 in the script, but used in Scene 13 in the film.)

Scene 10. This scene contains everybody's favorite shot in the movie. It's the amazing aerial view that first reveals the prison in all its bleak glory, with the army of prisoners streaming across the yard below to greet the arriving bus. It's a wonderfully cinematic moment, one that seems to suspend time even as it plunges us breathlessly into this new and horrible world…

…and boy, would I love to take credit for it, but you'll notice it's not even alluded to in the script. Truth is, it was production designer Terence Marsh's idea. On our very first scout to determine the viability of using the abandoned Ohio State Reformatory in Mansfield as our primary location, producer Niki Marvin, coexecutive producer David Lester, Terry Marsh, and I found ourselves abjectly freezing our butts off and picking sleet out of our teeth (real winters come as a nasty surprise if you've just flown in from California). Suddenly, Terry (two-time Academy Award winner and last of the soft-spoken gentlemen) blinked up at the sky and muttered something like: "This place would look smashing with an opening helicopter shot."

Six months later we were back again, this time with a veritable army of crew and trucks, desperately trying to get the shot in the can before lunch. This involved coordinating three major elements (and believe me, everybody's timing *had* to be perfect): the helicopter in the air, the bus on the ground, and the 500 extras in the yard. It didn't help that the copter could only go up (or the extras emerge from hiding) in the intermittent breaks between rain flurries.

The shot came off perfectly. It's even got the state flag of Maine snapping smartly in the breeze as if saluting Stephen King. It helps to have a great pilot (Bobby Z), a great aerial camera operator (Mike Kelem), intrepid assistant directors (John Woodward and Tom Schellenberg, who spent a month planning placement and movement of the prisoners in the yard as if diagramming the world's biggest football play), stout-hearted extras (the fine men of Mansfield and surrounding areas), and God or the universe on your side. Most of all, it helps to have a great idea to set all the madness in motion. Thanks, Terry.

Scenes 12 & 13. Due to the amazingly unpredictable weather in Ohio, it took us over a *week* to get this sequence fully shot. We needed overcast—not only for mood, but to match all the footage we'd already shot for Scene 10. The days of early summer in that region of Ohio generally *do* start out overcast, but it doesn't last long—it'll go from gray skies to bright sunshine fast enough to give you whiplash (we actually caught it on film a few times; you should see our ruined takes). In other words, every time we'd get started, we'd get only a few shots in the can before the sun came out again. From there, it would be a mad scramble to see what *else* we could shoot that day instead, which meant jumping ahead in the schedule to tackle a scene that could be shot in sunlight (and preferably had a lot of extras, since we had plenty on hand and on the payroll). This is how we shot all of Scene 36 (four solid pages of dialogue between Andy and Red the first time they meet) and all the exterior footage for Scenes 136 through 145 (convicts listening to Mozart). Finally, by being persistent and shooting 12 & 13 in small doses, we did manage to complete Andy's arrival at Shawshank under dismal gray skies.

Captain Hadley clubbing Andy in the back with his baton in Scene 12 proved arch and melodramatic during rehearsals (especially with the beating of Fat-Ass looming just a few scenes later), so we never bothered shooting it.

Those who delight in trivia might enjoy having me point out actor Brian Libby in the role of Floyd—he's the tall, gravel-voiced guy who kicks off Scene 13 by saying, "Takin' bets today, Red?" (He also delivers one of the audience's favorite lines in Scene 104: "Red, I do believe you're talking out of your ass.") The reason I single him out is that he's been in every film I've directed so far, starting with his excellent performance as The Prisoner in my Stephen King short *The Woman in the Room,* then continuing with his wryly comic turn as Earl the Embalmer in my made-for-cable movie *Buried Alive.* There's something Lee Marvin-ish about the guy that I love, though Stephen King insists he's got a "Neville Brand" quality. Whichever the case, I've been a big fan of Brian's from the get-go, so I try to find a role for him in everything I do. (Besides, I've come to think of him as my "good luck charm." And who says directors aren't superstitious?)

Scene 14. During shooting of this scene, it became apparent that the screenplay's suggestion that we watch *all* the new cons get hosed and deloused was ill-advised at best, horrendously protracted at worst. Why not do the intelligent thing and focus this humiliation and discomfort on our main character? By rethinking the scene a bit to include a simple time-jump—we cut from Hadley shouting "Unhook 'em!" to Andy stepping naked into the steel cage—we were able to do just that.

Scenes 15 & 16. Dropped during filming. These two scenes, though nice details, represent the kind of "expendable" (by which I mean *non-crucial* to the narrative coherency of the film) sequences that get tossed when you don't have enough hours in the day. In this case (as with most of what we didn't shoot) it's just as well—in tightening the film in the editing room, these scenes would certainly have hit the floor anyway.

Scene 17. I'll pause here to toot production designer Terence Marsh's horn again (it won't be the last time). Most people assume that the giant cellblock that appears in this film (first glimpsed in this scene) was merely a practical prison location. Not so. It was actually a *set* designed by Terry and built from scratch by his crew in a warehouse about a mile from the prison (the real cellblocks at the Ohio State Reformatory would have been impossible to light or shoot). It was an absolute marvel, one of the most magnificent sets I've ever seen: four stories high, 200 individual cells, cell doors that opened and closed on an air-pressure system (courtesy of propshop foreman Isadoro Raponi), the works. If I'd walked you blindfolded into that warehouse, then removed the blindfold, you'd have sworn you were on a real cellblock. It was that good.

More than just the cellblock, though, there was a stunning amount of work required to make the actual prison presentable for camera. Abundant modifications were necessary, thus many sets were built to reconfigure real exterior and interior locations (the prison library in its many incarnations, for example). But beyond even that, Terry and his crew did an amazing job of just putting that prison back *together.*

I mean, the place was *trashed* when we got there. Several winters with no heating had left countless strips of tattered paint dangling from *every* indoor surface (walking into that three-story high mess hall for the first time was like entering a vast cave with thousands of stalactites dangling overhead). Warden Norton's office, gorgeous as it looks on film, originally appeared as if somebody had detonated a powerful bomb in it. And I'll never forget the day I showed up during preproduction to discover Terry, unflappable as ever, making plans to restore the 10-ton chunk of prison wall that had fallen out onto the road during the night. (Talk about the Dutch boy plugging holes; Terry and his crew were kept busy trying to keep the dike from collapsing throughout the entire shoot.)

No sour grapes here, just my personal opinion: I do believe Terry Marsh was passed over for an Academy Award nomination because people didn't realize the challenge involved or recognize the magnitude and quality of his work; they simply assumed we walked into a real prison and started shooting. His work was simply too *seamless* to be noticed. I guess it's a compliment, in a weird way. (As Arthur C. Clarke is said to have once wryly observed: "*2001* did not win the Academy Award for makeup because the judges may not have realized the apes were human actors.")

Scenes 21 through 29. The thing I find interesting about this "Fat Ass gets clobbered" stretch of the film is that it demonstrates how very much *sound* plays a part in bringing a movie across. Somebody once said that a good portion of what you think you're *seeing* on screen is actually conveyed by the *sound* you're hearing. In this case, the scene works because of all the prisoners' voices you hear offscreen—the taunting, yelling, chanting, what have you. The truth is, we shot these scenes with a few dozen extras at most (including the guards), but you'd swear that massive 200-cell cellblock was *filled* with hardened lunatics. This is due to the amazing work done by Barbara Harris and her talented troupe of "loop group" actors performing these voices as separate and combined sound elements during postproduction, the further amazing work done by sound editor John Stacy and his team in assembling all those elements, and the final spectacular job done by dialogue mixer Bob Litt in laying all those sound elements in with the precision of a brain surgeon. (Another important contribution to this scene came from my good buddy David J. Schow, a fabulous writer who took pity on my brain-fried state during postproduction and knocked out several invaluable pages of additional offscreen lines for the prisoners to taunt and shout. Since we'd already shot our film's end credits, I never got a chance to thank him on screen, but maybe I can correct that omission by thanking him here.)

We did some local casting in Ohio for smaller "walk-on" roles (a fairly common practice which saves a production the trouble and expense of flying an actor in from Los Angeles or New York to speak a single line of dialogue). The guard who kicks off Scene 21 by shouting "Lights out!" is played by John Summers, a real-life guard who works at the new prison just up the road from the old one. (He worked at the old prison too, the one you see in the film, until its deactivation in 1990.)

The bit at the end of Scene 29 where the guards get Fat-Ass on the stretcher was dropped in favor of Hadley simply saying: "Call the trustees. Get this tub of shit down to the infirmary." Dramatically speaking, it simply felt right for the scene to *end* after he threatens the entire cellblock, rather than bogging down our screen time with stretcher-loading logistics. Besides, it struck me that having guards quickly rush in with a stretcher would have been a potential "Keystone Cops" moment (i.e., do you think they *always* follow Byron Hadley around with a stretcher just in case he gets in a bad mood and decides to wallop the bejeezus out of someone?)

Scenes 22 through 25. Though I would have loved to grab some footage of the other "new fish" in their cells (some great faces there), time did not allow. Still, I think the sequence cut together pretty well without them, which only goes to show that—when in doubt and racing the clock—if you shoot what you *know* you need (usually the principal characters), you can't go too far wrong.

Scene 32. In shooting any scene involving animals, a representative of the American Society for the Prevention of Cruelty to Animals will show up on your set to make sure you don't abuse or otherwise do something horrible to the critter involved (a laudable enough intent, given that filmmakers once had no compunction about indulging certain nasty practices like tripping horses with wires, etc.). So, naturally, the day we shot James Whitmore with the baby crow in his pocket, the ASPCA lady arrived to monitor our activities. Much to our surprise, we discovered she was there not only to protect the rights of the baby bird, but also of the *maggots* to be used in the scene. (I guess maggots are people too.) She decreed that no live worm be fed to the bird. Only a dead one would do. *One that died of natural causes.* My suggestion that we have the maggot autopsied to determine cause of death drew nothing but a blank stare. Patiently explaining that the maggots were actually waxworms purchased by the prop department at a local *bait shop* also cut us no slack. Apparently, the God-given right of any fisherman to blithely feed a waxworm to a steelhead bass is denied the Hollywood filmmaker and his baby crow, even when the Clock of Doom is ticking off $120,000 a day in production costs. Thank God we found a dead waxworm in the batch, or we might still be there.

Before the day was out, our intrepid grips had presented us with a tiny director's chair made out of matchsticks, just in case any of the waxworms needed a breather between takes.

Scene 33. Dropped during editing for reasons of length. A portion of this footage was used to replace Scene 35 in the film.

Scene 34. Based on his input during rehearsals, a portion of Mark Rolston's (Bogs) dialogue was modified here. I think Mark's subtler version is superior to what I wrote; it's more menacing and realistic.

Scene 35. Dropped during editing. Some footage from Scene 33 was used here instead. Additional voice-over by Red was added during post-production to provide a smoother transition.

Scene 36. The bit where Heywood zings the baseball at Andy's head didn't work very well, so we dropped it during editing.

I always point to this scene whenever people ask me if I rewrote any part of the script to accommodate the fact that Morgan Freeman was cast as a character originally written by Stephen King as a white Irishman. The answer is no. We even kept Red's line about his being Irish, which takes on an interesting and amusing new twist when spoken by Morgan (we shifted it to the end of the scene to better play the joke).

By the way, just to show you what a swell guy Morgan Freeman is, let me point out that he is playing catch throughout this scene. Though it lasts only a few minutes on screen, we spent an *entire day* shooting it. It didn't occur to me until much later how goddamn *sore* his arm must have gotten. (The last time I played more than half an hour of catch, my arm nearly fell off.) Though it had to hurt like hell, not once did he complain. He just kept tossing that ball and playing the scene.

Scenes 37 & 38. Dropped during editing for reasons of length.

Scenes 39 through 41. Here's a great example of something reading just fine in the script, but *really* not working on film. When editor Richard Francis-Bruce first cut this scene together, he added Red's voice-over as specified. The result was utter confusion. You were seeing one thing, listening to another, and completely unable to concentrate on either since the two stories didn't relate at all. The obvious solution was not to beg the question of how or why Andy had money. We scrapped the narration and just let the sequence play with Thomas Newman's excellent music.

Scenes 43 & 44. The bit at the end of the scene where Brooks relays a written thank-you note back to Red was dropped during filming in favor of Andy whispering his thanks to Brooks. Sending Brooks and that cart on a return trip to Red's cell would simply have consumed too much screen time.

Scene 47. This scene is the beginning of a longer "prison montage" (Scenes 48 through 52) detailing Andy's miserable day-to-day existence. While writing the script, I tossed a few vague ideas on the page here to kick things off, such as Andy working, eating, and shaping his rocks after lights-out. Kinda boring, when you stop and think. Besides, stuff like this is easy to write, but time-consuming to shoot. So what does a director do when he's up against the wall and fighting the clock? He decides he won't even bother. Instead, he'll steal a really nifty piece of footage he shot for Scene 31 (a dolly shot of guards doing the morning count) and uses it here instead. *Voilà.* A great visual to kick off our montage.

Scene 48. Since our story spans twenty years, I had my heart set on doing at least *one* snow shot somewhere in the film to help convey passage of time. But how does one do this in the middle of summer in Ohio? The answer, courtesy of special effects, was potato flakes. When cooked, it makes a hearty addition to any meal. But when dumped by the bucket-load through the spinning blades of a monstrous Ritter fan, it makes for some damn convincing snow.

Scene 49. Dropped during editing for reasons of silliness (with voice-over shifted to Scene 50). Besides, when viewed on film, it made Bogs out to be some sort of demented gay. This is contrary to what Stephen King or I intended. Both the novella and the film take pains to draw a distinction between a homosexual and a prison rapist. Why? Because there *is* a difference, a big one. According to sociologists, the prison rapist is seldom a homosexual in the outside world—what he is, is a damn *rapist.* When these scumbags are put behind bars, they continue doing what they do to whomever is handy. So let me state it one last time for the record: Bogs as a character does not represent homosexuality; he represents the predatory sexual violence of rape.

Scene 50. Voice-over scrapped to tighten the sequence.

Scene 51. Dropped during editing for reasons of length.

Scene 56. Dropped during editing for reasons of length. Voice-over shifted to Scene 57.

Scene 58. We had two weeks of acting rehearsals on location in Mansfield just prior to shooting. Though rehearsing may sound like a needless luxury to some, this scene is a strong argument in favor of it. Not only are rehearsals good for tweaking dialogue and performances, but they're *great* for spotting problem areas in the script. One such problem cropped up here, and I'm glad we caught it early, because it would have slowed us to a *crawl* trying to figure it out during filming.

So what's the big deal? Except for some minor dialogue changes, the scene seems to read exactly as it plays in the movie, right? Well, not exactly. Read it again, only this time with an eye toward timing. You'll notice the screenplay has Hadley and the guards completing their conversation about inheritance taxes—*after* which, the convicts trade a few whispered comments and Andy saunters over to tell Hadley a few things about IRS loopholes. Sure, it *reads* fine, but just try blocking it and you'll soon discover that the actor playing Hadley is left standing there with nothing to do once he's finished his dialogue except suffer awkwardly through one hell of a long pause waiting for Andy to get there.

This is the difference between writing a scene and blocking it. The director realizes that, for the scene to work, Andy has to get to Hadley just as soon as Hadley's dialogue ends. That means that the convicts' dialogue (along with Andy stepping away from the group) has to find a new home *earlier* in the scene—in other words, it has to be backed up and played *over* Hadley's dialogue so that the two conversations overlap. This way Andy can break away from his group and get to the guards by the time Hadley finishes talking. And because this is only a rehearsal, because the clock isn't yet ticking away the precious minutes of a costly shooting day, the director has all the time he needs to puzzle out which of Hadley's lines are expendable enough to be played under the convicts' dialogue. And that, in case anybody should ever ask, is the value of rehearsal.

Scene 59. We never shot this, because it seemed a better idea to cut straight from Scene 58 (Andy bargaining with Hadley) to Scene 60 (convicts drinking beer). This way we could stay focused on the *people* involved, rather than a bucket. Red's voice-over from this scene was shifted to Scene 60.

Scene 60. This is perhaps the best example of the *technical* aspect of shooting a film with voice-over in mind (at least *this* film; I'm not sure how other people have done it). I realized early on that many of the scenes we'd be filming would depend on Morgan Freeman's voice-over for timing (there's no point shooting a scene to be 30 seconds long if the voice-over lasts only 10). So we prerecorded *all* of Morgan's voice-over in a single session during preproduction to be available for playback on the set during filming (sort of like shooting a music video, where recorded music plays while the rock star lip-syncs the words). In other words, if a scene depended on precision timing with the voice-over, I'd ask Willie Burton, our location sound mixer, to play that bit of voice-over during the take for all to hear. (Later, during post, those sections of sound were replaced with clean narration.) In the case of this scene, it allowed for exact timing of: a) the camera move and assorted cons' reactions; b) Clancy Brown (Hadley) entering the shot to deliver his line, and; c) Morgan Freeman's glance to Tim Robbins.

Scene 61. A bit of dialogue (Red asks Andy if he's carved his name on his wall yet) was dropped from this scene during editing. When viewed on film, it didn't seem to us that Andy needed this line to motivate his actions in Scene 62.

Scenes 63 & 64. Here's an example of great ideas just waiting to happen, of pleasant surprises popping up when you least expect them, of turning disadvantages into strengths. You'll notice that the screenplay (as does Stephen King's story) has the convicts watching Ray Milland in *The Lost Weekend*. Our producer, Niki Marvin, approached Paramount Pictures about using a clip from that film. As it turns out, Paramount wanted a *lot* more money than we had budgeted, so Niki suggested we check out Columbia Pictures' film library instead (she figured they'd be more inclined to give us a price break, since they'd be releasing *Shawshank* domestically). Columbia faxed a list of their old films to us in Mansfield. I'll never forget the moment Niki looked up from scanning the titles and said, "Hey! There's a bunch of *Rita Hayworth* movies on this list! Let's use *Gilda,* for God's sakes!"

It's amazing, looking back on it, that it never dawned on us until that moment. *Of course we should put Rita Hayworth in the movie!* Creative choices don't get any better than that. All it took was a smart producer turning a disadvantage into a strength and recognizing the creative potential. Thanks, Niki.

Scene 67. Dropped during editing for reasons of length. Voice-over shifted to Scene 66.

Scenes 70 through 77. Here's an ambitious sequence that our schedule simply didn't allow me time to shoot. Given all the footage necessary to cut the sequence together (as well as the time-consuming stunts and effects), I believe I would have needed three full days to get everything in the can. As it was, I had a single afternoon. That meant thinking on my feet and coming up with the simplest solution. Obviously, the big high-fall stunt and the ancillary characters (Ernie and Red) were out of the question. I decided instead to focus the scene on Bogs and the guards. By having Bogs try to crawl from his cell and grab the railing, I could go to a simple side-angle view as he gets jerked back inside by the unseen guards. Though a compromise, I do think it proved a nice alternative—poor Bogs vanishes abruptly from view like some hapless swimmer in *Jaws*, leaving us staring at the deserted tier for punctuation.

Scene 78. Though it's written as one scene, I wound up shooting this as *two* scenes separated by a brief time-jump: a) Bogs gets wheeled to the ambulance; b) the ambulance pulls out to reveal Red and the gang watching from behind the fence. It simply felt more visually graceful! to do it that way. (That old ambulance was beautiful, but—like *every* period vehicle I've ever seen used in any movie—inevitably developed mechanical trouble. In this case, the engine block decided to crack, leaving us with a giant white paperweight instead of an ambulance. So here's what you're *not* seeing on screen as that ambulance departs: me and about half a dozen grips and electricians pushing that sucker from behind, trying to get up enough speed to send it coasting by itself through the shot. The group of us stopping was a sight, as we were all waving our arms for balance and trying not to fall on our noses into the camera's view. Let's credit Morgan Freeman for delivering his dialogue with a straight face.)

Scene 81. This was combined with Scene 82 for simplicity of shooting. Red was dropped.

Scenes 83 & 84. These were expendable and never shot.

Scene 85. The latter portion of this scene (the discovery of the sharpened screwdriver and the con being sent to solitary) was dropped during editing for reasons of length.

Scene 87. Dropped during editing for reasons of length.

Scene 91. The end of this scene was dropped during editing, because it made for a more graceful cut to Scene 92 when shortened.

Scene 92. During rehearsals, James Whitmore felt strongly that the casual profanity should be dropped from Brooks' dialogue in this scene. It's not because Jim's a prude; he actually had two excellent reasons. First, he pointed out that Brooks is of a much earlier generation which was not given to profaning casually. Second, he felt that by holding back the swearing here, it would make the scene where Brooks flips out and holds a knife to Heywood's throat (Scene 103) all the more shocking by virtue of the contrast in his language (the old boy's swearing up a *storm* in 103). Jim was right, of course. What else would you expect from an old pro like him?

Scene 97. The visual of the guards waiting in line was replaced during filming with an image of Andy preparing Warden Norton's taxes. I did this for two reasons. First, I thought that cutting from a shot of guards waiting in line to another shot of guards waiting in line would be visually repetitive and boring, possibly confusing. Second, I wanted to give Andy and Warden Norton some extra time on screen in this early part of the film to lay the groundwork for what follows. This seemed a good opportunity to do it, brief though it is.

Scene 98. An expendable scene that was never shot. Red's voice-over shifted to Scene 99.

Scene 99. Here's another real-life prison guard playing a small role in the film: Donald E. Zinn, doing a great job as the "Moresby Batter" getting his taxes done.

Scene 101. An expendable scene that was never shot. I knew early on that I wanted to drop this because it would needlessly slow the movie down. I *did* want the image of the chess piece being carved somewhere in the movie, though, so I used it as a detail in Scene 62.

Scene 103. The tail of this scene (Red comforting Brooks) was dropped during editing. It was stronger to end right after Heywood delivers the news about Brooks being paroled.

Scenes 105 & 106. Expendable scenes that were never shot.

Scene 108. It seemed a stronger creative choice *not* to have Red, Andy, and the other cons present when Brooks leaves the prison. It's sadder and more melancholy (and less obvious) to have the Shawshank guards being the only ones to see him off.

Scene 111. A prop-driven airliner? This is one of those goofy writer's touches you *know* will never wind up on screen even as you're writing it.

Scene 112. Dropped during editing for reasons of length.

Scene 113. Here's another example of production designer Terry Marsh's fabulous work. Brooks Hatlen's hotel room at the Brewster was actually a reworked office in the administration wing of the old prison.

Scene 121. This scene didn't work the first time we shot it, for two reasons. First, we shot it in broad sunlight, which didn't match the mood. Second, having *all* the cons present started to feel a bit *Little Rascals* to me (Spanky and Buckwheat and Alfalfa and Darla…shit, they were *always* in the club house together!). So, during filming, we reshot this as a very simple scene with only Andy and Red, placing them in the shadow of the prison to simulate gray overcast.

Scenes 122 through 126. I never had time to shoot this section of the film, for which I'll always have mixed feelings. The writer in me mourns its absence, because it's among my favorite sequences written. The director in me realizes it's probably just as well—since it isn't vital from a strictly narrative standpoint, I ultimately would have faced the tough decision of losing it in the editing room to tighten an already long movie. (As William Goldman so wisely observes in his excellent book *Adventures in the Screen Trade,* sometimes you have to kill your darlings…)

The absence of this sequence does put an interesting and different spin on the Brooks/Jake subtext. As Red notes toward the end of the film, "Some birds aren't meant to be caged." As written, neither Brooks nor Jake is that kind of bird; neither can survive on the outside. As filmed, however, Jake *can* survive, but Brooks can't. In a symbolic sense, Jake now represents Andy and Brooks represents Red. It's a subtle but fairly meaningful shift.

Scenes 127 & 128. Dropped during editing for reasons of length.

Scene 129. Some of the footage at the end of the scene (Andy opening boxes) was dropped during editing to tighten the sequence.

Scene 131. The action of Andy setting up the record player was never shot (it was obvious during filming that it would make for a very long scene).

Scene 134. Since it's not a scene that occurs in Stephen King's novella, I've been asked where the idea came from to have Andy broadcast Mozart throughout the prison. The answer is, I *love* music. *All* kinds, not just what they're dishing up this week on MTV. More to the point, I tend to write to music, because I find that it informs and infuses the creative process, sends my imagination wandering places it wouldn't normally go, gives me ideas, makes me *see* things. In this sense, I've had many cowriters, everyone from Duke Ellington to Hans Zimmer to...yes, Mozart. I happened to be listening to *The Marriage of Figaro* while writing this script, and the duet between Susanna and the Contessa simply insisted on being in the movie. As applied in the film, music represents freedom of the soul in the same way that the books in Andy's library represent freedom of the mind.

By the way, a *lot* of people have asked me where they can get that Mozart piece sung by those particular artists. If you're interested, the duet itself appears on the extraordinary *Shawshank Redemption* soundtrack written by Tom Newman and available from Epic Soundtrax (this is not a sleazy plug; it's simply a *great* movie score for which Tom was nominated for a Grammy and an Academy Award)—but if you want to hear even more of Mozart's sublime opera (and you should), rush out and grab a CD called *The Marriage of Figaro: Highlights*, with Karl Böhm conducting, from the Deutsche Grammophon label, CD stock number 429 822–2.

Scenes 136 through 143. The footage for this sequence was inevitably dictated by the location we chose. Though perfect in many ways, the Ohio State Reformatory lacked certain elements of the screenwriter's imagination (such as motor pool, kitchen, or license plate factory interior), so we picked the most interesting spots available.

Scene 146. Dropped during editing for reasons of pace.

Scene 147. All the dialogue spoken by Warden Norton and Captain Hadley through the glass door was improvised during blocking of this scene just prior to filming. More significantly, the punchline of the scene—Andy *turning up the volume* instead of shutting the record off as he's been ordered—was a stroke of genius on the part of Tim Robbins.

Scenes 148 & 149. Dropped during editing for reasons of length. Red's voice-over shifted to Scene 147.

Scene 150. Here's a good example of sometimes less-being-more where coverage of a scene is concerned, and I have our fabulous cinematographer Roger Deakins to thank for teaching me the lesson. While blocking this scene the day prior to filming it, I found myself at a loss for how to *shoot* it. For one thing, it's one of many "mess hall" scenes in the movie, and good luck figuring out how to make a bunch of guys sitting around a table visually different each time. For another, there are *eight* actors at that table, most with lines of dialogue to speak. What does one do? Shoot angles of *everybody?* That would have made for one very cutty scene, but more significant was the fact that I wouldn't have *time.* The schedule dictated getting the whole scene in the can before lunch. These were the dire, doom-laden thoughts which tormented me as I stood there listening to the actors run their lines—but then I glanced over and noticed Roger with a viewfinder to his eye, doing what I can only describe as a slow, sidling "Groucho walk." He obviously had something in mind, and it obviously had something to do with a camera move. After Groucho-walking through a few more rehearsals, Roger suggested boiling what I thought might be as many as ten setups down to *two.* How? By starting off with a master of the entire table that slowly moves into a tight closeup of Tim Robbins, then shooting a reverse angle that moves into a closeup of Morgan Freeman.

More than a concession to our time restraints, Roger's idea was the smartest creative choice that could have been made. In fact, it's one of my favorite scenes in the movie for its visual economy and grace, and it illustrates the value of a filmmaker (in this case, Roger) thinking like a *storyteller.* By starting wide on the table and slowly letting all the peripheral characters drop away, we focused the scene exactly where it belonged—on Andy and Red. It's *their* scene. Everything else is superfluous. It was a great lesson for me to learn. (I adopted the same kind of thinking in shooting Scene 161, resulting in another one of my favorite scenes in the movie.)

Scene 152. I'll use this as a quick example of what we call "shoe leather," which is an editing room term for superfluous shots of people walking somewhere (often entering or leaving a scene). You always need a lot less of it than you think. Trust me on this; there's nothing quite as boring as watching people walk somewhere for no reason. That's why Red doesn't enter this scene as written—it's a bit of shoe leather that hit the cutting room floor.

Scene 161. My producer, Niki, spent months insisting we didn't have time to shoot this scene. She was right, considering I'd planned something like ten camera setups for it during preproduction (I figured I'd need various shots of the warden, the journalists, the convicts, etc.). Besides the time factor, we couldn't afford to pay for one more big day in terms of the background actors needed. Still, this was *not* an expendable scene. The narrative was vital to the audience's comprehension. We *needed* it.

As the end of our shooting schedule loomed ever nearer, I started playing a mental game with myself. It's sort of like *Name That Tune,* only the object isn't how few bars you need to identify the song, it's how few shots you need to shoot the scene. Taking a cue from the Roger Deakins School of Visual Economy (the lesson I learned while shooting Scene 150), I decided to boil the sucker down to *two* setups: a) an overhead tracking shot of the reporters that tilts up into a single of Warden Norton speechifying, and; b) a simple, quick cutaway shot of three photographers taking pictures from the crowd. I had Niki schedule it at the end of the same day we were shooting Captain Hadley being arrested (Scene 259), thus making use of background actors already on payroll.

I love the way the scene turned out. It's got far more energy and interest than if I'd shot a bunch of angles and strung them together. Plus, I have to admit, you get a wacky charge out of kicking the *schedule's* ass for a change (hell, I can name that tune in *two* shots!).

Scenes 162 & 163. Expendable scenes we didn't have time to shoot. It's another one of those sequences that the writer in me regrets not having on screen, but the director in me is a bit more philosophical about (see explanation of 122 through 126.)

Scene 164. Here's another one we had to get in the can before lunch. That meant simplifying all the peripheral action, eliminating the injured man, and focusing the scene on Norton and Grimes. (Besides, good luck finding anything resembling a swamp in Ohio during the summer…)

Scene 166. An expendable scene that was never shot.

Scene 169. In this shot, you can catch a glimpse of Warden Dennis Baker, the actual real-life warden of the new Ohio State Reformatory (which was built just up the road from the old one). Warden Baker decided to be a good sport and join us on the set as an extra one day. He had one request, though—he wanted to play a convict. He's the black gentleman sitting on the bus right behind actor Gil Bellows, who plays Tommy.

Scenes 170 through 173. We never shot these scenes, thank goodness. They would have been large scenes to mount, with the only result being more "shoe leather" to eliminate in the cutting room. Red's voice-over was shifted from 173 to 169.

Scenes 175 & 176. To ease the shooting schedule, I combined these two separate scenes into one.

Scene 177. Here's another scene I'm sorry we didn't have time to shoot. I'm sorry because the young actress we hired for the role, Tracy Needham, would have been *wonderful!* Boy, did *she* kick ass in her audition! (Sorry, Tracy, but the schedule got us again. I hope to make it up to you one day.) Red's voice-over was shifted to Scene 178.

Scenes 179, 180, 183. Expendable scenes that were never shot.

Scene 184. Dropped during editing for reasons of length.

Scene 186. Somewhere along the way, I got it in my head that this scene would be more evocative *without* the star of the movie in it. Something about the minute examination of Andy's *empty* cell felt right to me, a way of revealing small glimpses of the man's character based on the personal possessions he's accumulated through the years and the photos he's chosen to hang on the walls (I guess this would be the voyeuristic equivalent of going through somebody's underwear drawer when they're not home). Thankfully, Tim Robbins was not at all offended that I chose to exclude him here.

Scene 188. Tommy's final reaction as scripted in this scene (dropping the Coke and whispering "Oh my God") proved far too melodramatic, so we didn't shoot it.

Scene 193. What do you do when you have eight guys in a scene, a lot of dialogue, and only a few hours to shoot? Slap the camera on a Steadicam and get the whole thing in one shot. This is another example of a scene working out better with less-is-more thinking. (God bless the inventors of the Steadicam. I don't know how movies were made without them.)

Scene 194. An expendable scene that was never shot.

Scenes 202 & 203. These were never shot (see 204 for explanation).

Scene 204. Here's an example of the actor's instinct proving better than the writer's. There was something about this scene that bothered Tim Robbins from the very first rehearsal: *he thought the location was wrong.* Since this is Andy's lowest point in the story, he argued, then surely the scene should take place in solitary confinement instead of Norton's office. Tim was right. Having the scene take place in as mundane a setting as an office was not only less interesting and repetitive of what came before, but—by dint of so casual a setting—it put Andy and Norton on too much of an equal footing at this point in the story. However, by having Norton come to see Andy in the "hole," we have the perfect and logical setting for the power-play taking place, for the threats and ultimatums. It puts Andy in his place and *keeps* him there, showing him at the lowest point of his subjugation. It was a great idea, and by far the best creative choice. Thanks, Tim.

Scene 207. Dropped during editing for reasons of length.

Scene 210. An expendable scene that was never shot.

Scene 213. We never shot Andy polishing the chess piece. The focus of this moment, the weight of this scene, had to be the rope hidden under the pillow. (Besides, enough with the rocks already! We'd seen plenty of them in the movie by now!)

Scene 215. Here's another real-life prison guard doing a great job playing a guard in the movie—Chuck Brauchler, who turns and hollers: "Man missing on tier two!"

Scene 216. I dropped this during shooting for two very good reasons; one practical, the other creative. On the practical side, the set we were shooting on was *so* small that there was no way on earth to reveal the entire cell (one couldn't just back the camera up, or use a wide enough lens, to get the whole thing into frame). On the creative side, I realized that cutting straight from 215 to 217 (from Haig's stunned face to Norton opening the shoebox) would delay the revelation that Andy has vanished from his cell in a way that would heighten the audience's pleasure and anticipation.

Scenes 218 & 219. I combined these two scenes into one. I believe it plays better entirely on the cellblock tier; it's funnier and more direct.

Scenes 222 through 227. This has always been one of my favorite sequences in Stephen King's story; it made me laugh till tears were rolling down my cheeks when I first read it. And because it's also the movie's best example of a terrifically written sequence dropping dead on screen with a dull thud, it points up the fundamental difference between a book and a movie. Written fiction and film are two different languages, and sometimes things just don't translate. What was excruciatingly funny on the printed page became excruciatingly labored and protracted on screen. My editor Richard and I spent weeks trying to figure out *why* it didn't work, recutting it numerous times to try and make the pieces fit. Finally, it dawned on me that the sequence didn't work for one reason—*it didn't belong in the movie.* Why? Because once we see Norton discover a tunnel behind the poster, once we realize that Andy has actually by-God *escaped,* we want the movie to *deal* with that revelation. We want to see what happens next, where Andy went, how he pulled it off. What we *don't* want is to go off the subject entirely, to take a leisurely two-and-a-half-minute detour down an airshaft at the end of a rope with a character we've never met.

When I asked Richard to remove the sequence entirely—which meant going straight from Scene 221 (the warden's stunned face peering down the tunnel) to Scene 228 (the state police cars rocketing up the road)—this section of the movie sprang to life with an energy and momentum that had been completely absent before. From a narrative standpoint, it was the right decision to make. (Apologies to Anthony Lucero, the actor who played Rory, for cutting him out of the film. My other regret is that you never got a chance to see the footage of Morgan *laughing*. My God, the man went on for over two minutes, tears rolling down his face and barely able to breathe, leaving the viewer just as helpless. It was a wonderful performance.)

Scene 228. You see in the movie exactly what the screenplay describes: a rural road leading toward Shawshank Prison in the distance. What you *don't* see on screen is the fact that the only rural-looking road on a direct line of sight with the old prison is actually the *driveway* of the new prison just up the way (if the camera had panned even a few degrees to the left or right, you would have seen the perimeter fencing).

Scene 231. This was combined during filming with 233. Red's voice-over in 232 and 233 was shifted around a bit for a smoother flow.

Scene 234. The tail of this scene (Andy diving into bed as the guard strolls past) was never shot.

Scenes 236 through 238. Dropped during editing for reasons of length.

Scenes 239 & 240. Expendable scenes that were never shot.

Scene 241. This image seemed visually jarring during this sequence, so it was dropped during editing. Red's voice-over was shifted to Scene 242.

Scene 243. Dropped during editing for pace. Red's voice-over shifted to 244.

Scene 249. This scene is obviously much more elaborate in the script than in the film. Let's blame the clock again, because I had very little time to shoot it. (If there's one thing in the movie I could go back and improve, I'd get at least one or two more angles of Andy climbing down the shaft.) Also, because a ceramic sewer pipe is a hell of a lot thicker and sturdier than I imagined when writing, Andy's dinky little rock hammer was replaced with a handy chunk of concrete as the tool of choice for believably breaking the pipe open.

Scene 253. It was my editor Richard's wonderful inspiration *not* to reveal Andy's face in this scene, but to hold off showing him until 254.

Scene 255. For the sake of pace, I eliminated the second half of this scene during editing (the newspaperman jumping up to summon his reporters). Since that also eliminated the door with the words *PORTLAND DAILY BUGLE* on the glass, I compensated by adding an offscreen woman's voice answering a telephone with: "Good morning, Portland Daily Bugle." (This tighter version also improved the joke of suddenly cutting to Warden Norton's newspaper hitting the desk in the very next scene.)

Scene 256. While blocking this scene for filming, Roger Deakins made the brilliant suggestion of simply having the newspaper slap down into frame, thereby eliminating all the "shoe leather" of Norton entering the office and going to the desk.

Scene 264. During filming, I decided to simplify our shooting day by eliminating the D.A. and state troopers from this scene.

It became apparent early in pre-production that the physical layout of this room (placement of the desk versus that of the safe) would make it impossible for Norton's "blood and brains" to spatter on the sampler as written (which is just as well; this Scorsese-like effect would have clashed terribly with the more oblique approach I found myself using in depicting the violence throughout the rest of the film). Since the desk would be right in front of the windows, I decided instead to have a pane of glass blow out behind him. (Even though I toned down Norton's suicide substantially from what was written in the script, I was surprised when a few people in our test audience complained about this scene being too "graphic." Again, it just goes to show how compelling sound effects can be. If you examine it closely, you won't actually *see* anything graphic or gory when Norton shoots himself—no squibs were used on the actor, no gun was ever fired, no blood was sprayed all over the room. What you *do* see is an actor press a gun under his chin, a quick image of a window shattering, and a closeup of a gun hitting the floor. Once you add the sound effects of a gunshot and glass breaking, you've convinced some folks in the audience they actually *saw* something that they didn't.)

Scene 267. This, along with Scenes 298 & 299 (Andy and Red reunite on the beach at the end of the movie), was shot on our final day of principal photography on Saint Croix in the U.S. Virgin Islands (doubling for Mexico). I love this scene—the aerial shot has a wonderful, sweeping sense of freedom—but it also contains the worst continuity error in the movie. Though nobody's ever mentioned noticing it, the fact is we have Andy driving down to Mexico in 1966 behind the wheel of a Pontiac GTO circa *1969*. Our intrepid and resourceful transportation coordinator, David Marder, had arranged for a 1965 convertible Mustang to be shipped over from Miami for the shoot, but the owner of that car balked at the last moment. With the crew's arrival imminent, David scrambled to find a suitable replacement there on the island. What he found was the '69 GTO. (Beautiful car, even if it is a few years off.)

Scene 268. This illustrates the advantage of having really terrific actors. The story that Heywood is telling, plus all the reactions around the table, was completely unrehearsed and improvised. Bill Sadler, the superb actor who plays Heywood, just dove right in and worked that mess hall table like a conductor works an orchestra. The other actors gave right back, providing a lovely texture of camaraderie. For this reason, it's one of my favorite scenes in the movie.

Scene 269. The saddest thing we discovered at the old Ohio State Reformatory was the small pauper's graveyard that lay just outside the walls. This was the burial ground for those convicts who died in prison but didn't have families to claim their bodies. Sadder still, the headstones did not bear the *name* of the deceased, only his *number.* (As Bill Sadler observed, they didn't give a guy his identity back even *after* he died.) As evocative a detail as this graveyard was, I spent most of the shoot trying to figure out a way to work it into the movie. This scene gave me the perfect opportunity—given the context and Red's frame of mind, I think it strikes a haunting chord of melancholy and loss.

Scenes 270 through 273. Another sequence we didn't have time to shoot. Of all the scenes that fell victim to the schedule, this is the one I regret most. No, it's *not* vital to the narrative, and I suppose the movie doesn't really suffer from its lack. But, speaking as a writer, I thought it was my best work in the script (it was certainly the riskiest, and sometimes the riskiest stuff winds up being the most interesting). If I could have captured on film what I put down on the page…well, frankly, it might not have worked at all. Then again, it might have been sublime. We'll never know.

Scene 277. Dropped during editing for reasons of length.

Scene 278. An expendable scene that was never shot.

Scene 281. The Beatles cue was dropped (see 282 through 286 for explanation).

Scenes 282 through 286. The practice of "test-screening" generally gets a bad rap from filmmakers (and many movie buffs), but here's a great argument in favor of it. Yes, it is the most nerve-wracking night of your life. You're showing the very "work print" that your editor has dragged through the Steenbeck a zillion times; it's got scratches galore, color mismatches, temporary sound with a monaural mix, music borrowed from other soundtracks, tape splices jumping through the projector gate every time you cut to another shot—basically, everything you *don't* want an audience to see. Still, though you suffer through every second of it, the truth is you *don't* know how a film's going to play until you're trapped in a theater surrounded by real live moviegoers reacting to every moment of the film as it occurs on the screen before them. An audience, when observed closely, becomes an organic creature—I swear, you can *feel* them breathing, *sense* their mood, *taste* their reactions. It lets you see your own movie with new eyes. More to the point, it makes you *painfully* aware if something isn't working…

…which brings us to 282 through 286. It was an amazing experience to sit through these scenes with a live audience. They were good scenes, don't get me wrong. They played beautifully in and of themselves (especially 282, with Red checking out the women; hell, the audience *loved* that scene). But here's the odd contradiction: though the audience enjoyed what they were seeing scene by scene, the *sequence itself* made them terribly impatient. Why? *Because it spent three minutes telling them something they already knew.* They *knew* Red was institutionalized; they *knew* he wouldn't make it on the outside. And why shouldn't they? Not only was all that subtext and groundwork laid earlier in the movie with Brooks Hatlen (James Whitmore), but Red himself stated it outright in 205. So by the time Morgan Freeman entered the same hotel room in 279 and glanced up to see "Brooks Was Here" carved into the ceiling beam, the audience understood. They *believed*. And having believed, they now wanted to see Red go to that tree with the long rock wall. They wanted to know how the movie would end.

It shows that moviegoers can sometimes be far more intuitive than a filmmaker thinks. Sometimes they get three steps ahead, so you have to catch up. Though the scenes themselves were fine, eliminating 282 through 286 brought the entire end of the movie into focus. It was like extracting an irritating burr from the audience's side. (In this sense, it was not unlike losing 222 through 227, where the young guard is lowered down the shaft after Andy has escaped.)

Scenes 287 & 288. Since the object of Red's upcoming quest would be a hayfield "with a big oak at the north end," I always knew I wanted him searching the countryside with a compass in his hand. It occurred to me during filming that adding this compass to the pawnshop window might be a nice detail, providing a visual and thematic counterpoint to the guns on display. Symbolically speaking (not to get too artsy-fartsy about it), I thought "guns versus compass" might reflect Red's torn state of mind as he teeters between despair and hope. In 288, when we see him in his hotel room with the compass in his hand, we know he's leaning (temporarily at least) toward hope.

Scene 292. I decided while filming to shoot a version where the name "Red" *isn't* written on the envelope. I'm glad I did; it worked out much better delaying for even those few extra seconds the revelation that the "mystery object" is actually a message from Andy.

Also, during his examination of the mystery object, Red glances around on two separate occasions as if fearful of being observed. This funny and poignant bit of "convict's paranoia" was an inspired and insightful ad-lib by Morgan Freeman.

Scene "292A". I've put this scene number in quotes, because it doesn't actually exist in the script you've read (though it appears as a handwritten addition to the script supervisor's continuity draft). The scene I'm referring to occurs in the film between 292 and 293, and it consists of a lyrical shot of Morgan Freeman crossing a sun-dappled field after having read Andy's letter. The reason I single it out is that—along with the aerial view of the prison in Scene 10—it seems to be *everybody's* favorite shot in the movie. What makes it unique, what elevates it from nice to breathtaking, is the fact that countless grasshoppers are bursting from the alfalfa stalks all around Red, taking to the air with wings that literally glow in the late afternoon sun.

It's a hell of a shot, *my* personal favorite, but it certainly wasn't anything we planned. (Can you picture trying to train a bunch of grasshoppers?) We'd chosen that location months earlier, which gave my genius production designer (yes, Terry Marsh) and his stalwart crew plenty of time to ready the site for filming. A deal was struck with the farmer who owned the land, the existing alfalfa was harvested, and Terry's do-or-die gang of art department gonzos proceeded to build that damn wall *stone by stone,* laying every inch of it in *by hand.* (You didn't think we just *found* that wall, did you? What God or the universe does not provide, the art department must.) Stephen King described the wall as "right out of a Robert Frost poem." Well, I think Terry and his pirates did both King *and* Frost proud. I have no idea how many truckloads of rock they carted in before all was said and done (I never had the heart to ask), but having once worked in the art department, I can assure you it was an awesome task.

The theory was, once the wall was in place, the next crop of alfalfa would grow in, thereby providing us the perfect location when we came back to shoot those scenes months later. And the theory was correct. The planning and hard work paid off, the location was spectacular...

...with the unexpected bonus that, apparently, late summer in Ohio is grasshopper breeding season. The new alfalfa was swarming with them. I mean, you couldn't take two steps without those suckers scattering into the air. As we went through our day's filming, the thought of those grasshoppers kept tormenting me. *If only we could get them on film...*

Let's go to the blow-by-blow. Finally the day's work is complete. I glance at my watch. There's still twenty minutes left on the clock. I scan the fields. There's a perfect view to the west, with that magic late afternoon sun slanting in over a darkened treeline. I ask Roger Deakins, our cinematographer, if we can squeeze in one more quick setup. I describe the shot. Before you know it, there's a mad scramble to get it done, elbows flying as grips lay dolly track and the camera team loads film. This is the fun time, the no-pressure time when all the real work is done and everybody gets into the spirit of grabbing one last bonus shot just for the hell of it...

Camera's set. I'm seeing grasshoppers leaping and bounding perfectly as Morgan Freeman is escorted out into the field by our second-second assistant director, Mike Greenwood (why they aren't just called *third* assistant directors, I'll never know).

Morgan is positioned on his start-mark per my shouted instructions. Mike ducks out of frame, vanishing like a shadow. The camera rolls. Action! Morgan starts walking across that field just as lyrically as anyone could ever want...

...*and not one single miserable grasshopper pops so much as a twitching antenna into view.* The reason hits me upside the head like a two-by-four: all the little critters were scared out of Morgan's path when he and Mike first trudged out there (shit, and I *watched* them fleeing!). I yell cut and glance at my watch. Minutes left to go before union overtime kicks in. I shout for Morgan to hurry back to his start-mark, which he gamely does. Suddenly, before the startled eyes of cast and crew, lunatic director goes charging into the alfalfa field, hollering and doing the boogie, trying to scare those recalcitrant insects back into Morgan's path. I'm a beater flushing the lion! I'm Peter O'Toole in *The Stunt Man*! I will not be denied my grasshoppers! Thank God the ASPCA lady ain't here or she'd kick my ass for frightening the poor little darlings!

Roll camera! Action! Morgan starts to walk and—lo and behold!—grasshoppers fountain into the air, dozens and dozens of them, rimmed with light and glowing like faeries, a veritable grasshopper kaleidoscope! Cut! Print!

It just goes to show that, sometimes, what the art department does not provide, God or the universe will. You just have to be paying attention.

Scenes 298 & 299. The dialogue in 299 played fairly nicely on the page, but *stank* on screen. When spoken, these lines not only trampled the clarity and emotion of the moment, they had a cloying "golly-gee-ain't-we-cute" quality that would have sent you and everybody else screaming from the theater. Never before in motion picture history has a movie benefited more from leaving two simple lines of dialogue reeking like dog turds on the cutting room floor. Trust me.

Since it's not in Stephen King's original story, I get asked all the time about the finale on the beach. Most people love this ending, though there are a few purists in the crowd who would have preferred ending with King's image of the bus going down the road. Either way, folks have wanted to know whose idea it was, the reasoning behind it. Truth is, my first draft of the script *didn't* have this scene; it ended on the bus exactly as King's story does. However, the fine folks at Castle Rock (primarily Liz Glotzer, our patron saint) suggested that the audience would want to see Andy and Red *reunite* at the end after all the struggle and misery we've put these characters through. Though I was skeptical, I wasn't convinced Castle Rock was *wrong.* So I wrote the added scene, knowing that if it didn't work on film I could always leave it out of the movie.

Once we cut the sequence together in the editing room, we all started falling in love with it. (My editor Richard was particularly voluble on the subject: "Are you nuts? Ya gotta have it in the movie! Look at the smile on Morgan's face! It's great!") Nevertheless, I was still on the fence about using it, still a bit cautious. I wanted to see how the ending would play with a real audience before making a firm decision. The night of our first test-screening, I had my answer—they *loved* it. They wept, they cheered. More to the point, on the test cards they filled out, well over 90 percent of the audience singled this out as among their favorite scenes in the movie (the other favorite was Scene 60, with the convicts drinking beer on the roof).

Who was I to argue with those kinds of results? I think there's a difference between pandering to an audience and giving them something they love. Besides, as I said, I'd started falling in love with it myself. Looking back on it now, I wouldn't have it any other way. Liz Glotzer was right about it providing emotional catharsis. But even more than that, in a purely cinematic sense, I think it gives the movie a tremendous sense of closure. By ending with that final image, we've brought the viewer on a full journey that begins in tight claustrophobia defined by walls and concludes where the horizon is limitless; the movie has traveled fully from darkness to light, from coldness to warmth, from colorlessness to a place where only color exists, from physical and spiritual imprisonment to total freedom (which is the very thing I wanted to convey in 271 & 272, the dream sequence I never got the chance to shoot). Bottom line is, I think it's a magical and uplifting place for our characters to arrive at the end of their long saga...

Our final day of shooting on St. Croix—the camera copter makes a practice run with pilot Bobby "Z" Zajonc at the controls, while cinematographer Roger Deakins and first assistant director John Woodward stroll out across the sand.

STORYBOARDS

S tudents often ask about "storyboarding," which is the process of previsualizing a
film with a succession of drawings reminiscent of a comic book. How much value
does it provide in planning the shoot? When is it necessary, or when is it not?

I'm sure you'd get a different answer from every filmmaker you ask. I believe the
only hard-and-fast rule in filmmaking is that there *are* no hard-and-fast rules—there's
only instinct, and what works for you. Speaking subjectively, I do find storyboards
quite valuable, but only where *physical* sequences are concerned. By "physical," I
don't necessarily mean slam-bang action or effects scenes alone (for which I believe
they are vital), but also for scenes that involve more visual than verbal aspects of
storytelling—especially if that involves logistical challenges for the production.

For example, Andy's arrival at Shawshank Prison is not what one would classify
as an "action scene." Nevertheless, given the physical challenge of the sequence (a
giant prison, 500 extras, nearly a dozen lead actors, a bus, and an ambitious helicopter shot), I had to walk onto that set knowing that we'd be getting all the angles
necessary to cut together a coherent and creatively satisfying sequence later on.
Moreover, my *crew* needed to know the shot-by-shot requirements in order to plan
effectively. (Believe me, there's nothing worse than standing around on the set wast-
ing your shooting day trying to figure out where to put the camera.)

When it comes to purely *verbal* sequences, however, I question the value of storyboarding. By "verbal," I mean fairly straightforward scenes of actors exchanging dialogue. The quantity and nature of the angles is inevitably determined by the director
and cinematographer (often with input from the script supervisor) as a result of blocking and rehearsing the scene with the actors. Based on where your performers stand,
walk, turn, or sit, you figure out what angles you need and you shoot them (the slang
term for this, most often used by your wiseguy assistant director, is "carving up the

scene"). I really see no point in drawing pictures of this sort of thing, as most verbal scenes consist of speaking faces—besides, no matter what you decide in advance, the actors will always have their own ideas about where to stand, walk, turn or sit. And that's as it should be—they're actors after all, not chess pieces. (Again, let me stress all of this as a highly *subjective* view—if you feel storyboarding your verbal scenes will help you shoot your movie more effectively, by all means *do* it. Ultimately, there's no amount of planning that can ever be considered wasted.)

Storyboards come in all shapes and sizes. Some are very basic thumbnail sketches with stick figures, while others are more elaborate and fleshed out. Some directors prefer drawing the boards themselves (I understand Brian DePalma does his on computer, using a storyboarding program). Others prefer using a professional artist, which is the most common method, and the one that makes most sense to me. The process involves sitting with the artist (and the cinematographer, whenever I can pry him loose from his preproduction duties) and talking through the scenes, trying to imagine the shots that would best convey the story. I try to describe the images I have in mind. The artist listens, makes suggestions, and draws. The result, hopefully, is a blueprint that everybody in the production can study, understand, and use as a guide in committing the sequence to film.

Allow me one final observation, which, though related, goes well beyond the issue of drawing storyboards. One can visually conceptualize a movie *anywhere*—office, living room, you name it—but I find the most valuable place, if at all feasible, to be the actual location where filming will occur. The one thing I can be certain of is that the location will *always* be different than I imagined, and will consequently make its own demands on the way the scene is filmed. (Sometimes a location has the *final* say.) This is why I try to squeeze as much of my preproduction time as possible into visiting the locations with my cinematographer, discussing endlessly the various angles we might use in filming a given sequence the day we show up with the actors. For me, the time I spend "walking the sets" during prep is the most valuable time I can invest (it saves a stunning amount of time later when we're shooting), and if I can have the storyboard artist with me at those locations, so much the better.

The two most extensive of our boarded sequences follow; one of them appears in the movie, and one of them does not (at least not in its completely storyboarded form). They were drawn by artist Peter von Sholly, whom I met back in 1986 when he was boarding *Nightmare on Elm Street 3: Dream Warriors* for director Chuck Russell. Chuck and I both use Pete every chance we get, because he's got a wonderful facility for rendering (and helping to visualize) a scene. In viewing his work, I'm sure you'll recognize the prison as it appears in the film—obviously, Pete spent time with me in Ohio, tailoring the boards to our locations. Enjoy his work.

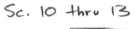

RED EXITS DOOR ...

PAN HIM RIGHT...

HE CLIMBS THE STAIRS...

... UP INTO YARD .

STEADICAM RED FROM
TOP OF STAIRS TO HIS
BUDDIES...

FOLLOW THEM INTO YARD.
THEY TURN AT SOUND OF
AIR HORN AND START
TOWARD MAIN GATE...

WHONK,
WHONK!

ADDITIONAL ANGLE FOR
VOICE-OVER COVERAGE!
LONG LENS SHOT OF
RED AND GROUP WALKING
TOWARD CAMERA (SHOOT
VARIOUS SPEEDS SLO-MO)!

WE PAN THE ARRIVING BUS...

ANGLE TURNS INTO HELICOPTER SHOT AS BUS PROCEEDS UP THE DRIVEWAY...

SHOT KEEPS GOING! CAMERA RISES UP OVER THE PRISON...

SWOOPING OVER TURRETS...

CONT.

CONT.

REVEALING THE YARD
AND CONS BELOW...

CAM
SWINGS AROUND

AND KEEPS GOING...

SWINGING LATERALLY OUT
OVER THE PRISON WALL...

...TO REVEAL THE BUS
COMING UP THE ROAD.

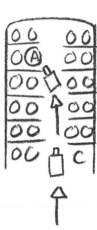

DOLLY (OR STEADICAM)
down aisle of bus
for shot of Andy.

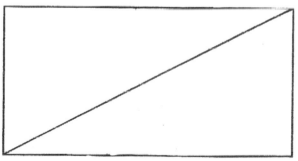

Sc. 10 thru 13

page 6

CLICK!

GATE UNLOCKED.
BUS PULLS IN.

STEADICAM RED AND
GANG TO BLEACHERS.
THEY SETTLE IN TO
WATCH.

WALL + GATE

BUS

166

GUARDS RUSH FROM
ROOF TOWER...

STEADICAM FORWARD
AND BETWEEN THEM...

...FOR HIGH ANGLE VIEW
AS BUS PULLS IN.

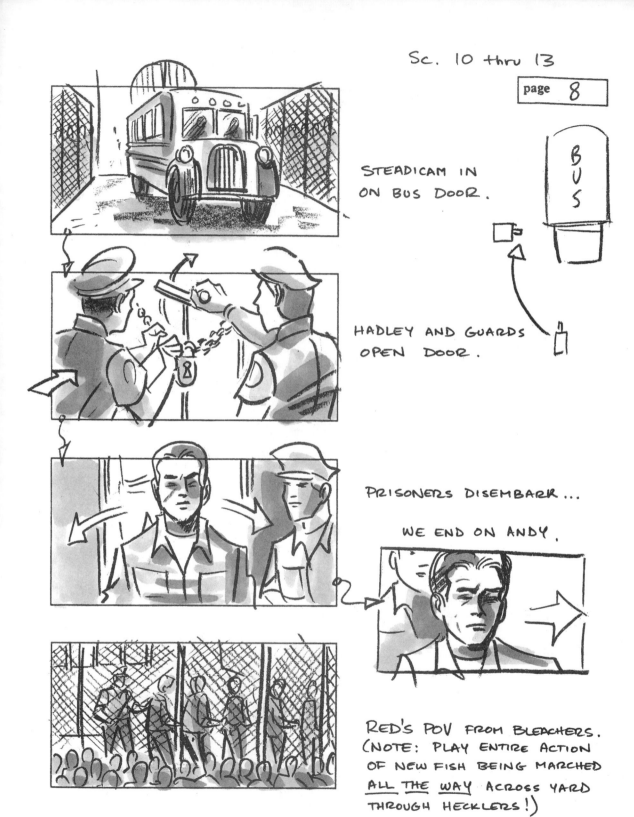

Sc. 10 thru 13

STEADICAM IN
ON BUS DOOR.

HADLEY AND GUARDS
OPEN DOOR.

PRISONERS DISEMBARK...

WE END ON ANDY.

RED'S POV FROM BLEACHERS.
(NOTE: PLAY ENTIRE ACTION
OF NEW FISH BEING MARCHED
ALL THE WAY ACROSS YARD
THROUGH HECKLERS!)

RED AND GANG:

VARIOUS SINGLES AND
GROUPINGS FOR COVERAGE
OF DIALOGUE.

ANDY (AND NEW FISH) POV:
OF CONS SHOUTING INSULTS
AND SHAKING THE FENCE.

STEADICAM LEADS ANDY
ENTIRELY ACROSS YARD.
(NOTE: GET SAME COVERAGE
OF "FAT-ASS" AND A FEW
OTHER INTERESTING FACES!)

ANDY LOOKS UP, AWED
BY THE BUILDING.

ANDY POV:

MOVING FORWARD...

TILTING UP...

BEING SWALLOWED BY
THE BUILDING...

...AND INTO DARKNESS!

END OF SEQUENCE

"BOGS TAKES A FALL" [Sc. 69 thru 77]

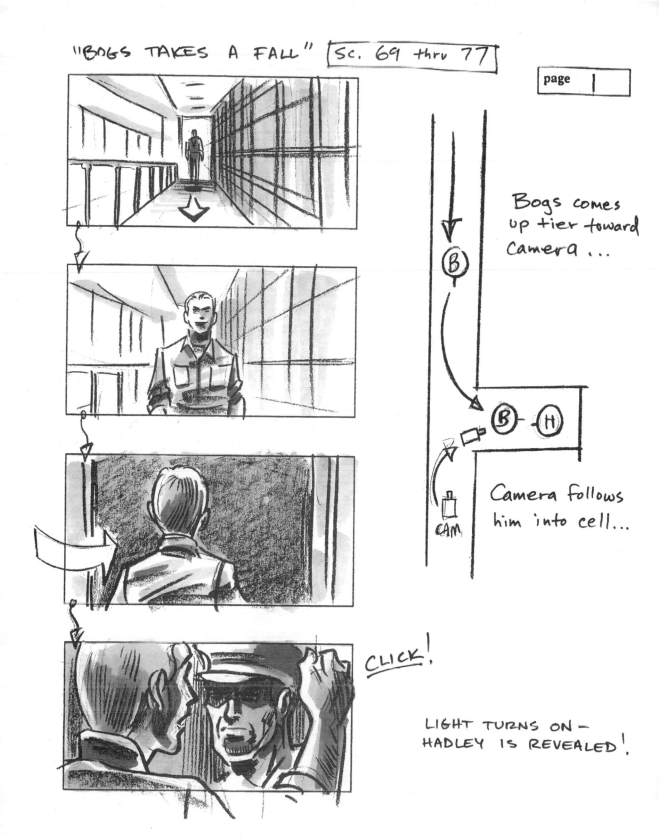

Bogs comes up tier toward Camera...

Camera follows him into cell...

CLICK!

LIGHT TURNS ON — HADLEY IS REVEALED!

MERT

MERT STEPS INTO FRAME
BEHIND BOGS...

OH OH...

HADLEY RAMS BATON
INTO BOGS' GUT!

BOGS DROPS TO FLOOR ...

BEATING BEGINS!

LOW ANGLE OF
HADLEY AND MERT ...

WIDE ANGLE FROM
ACROSS CELLBLOCK ...

RED DARNING SOCK ...

TILT UP AS HE REACTS
TO STRANGE SOUNDS...

PUSH IN AS RED COMES
OUT OF HIS CELL...
(NOTE: THIS IS OUR
MASTER OF RED LOOKING
FOR SOURCE OF SOUNDS.)

WINDOW
BG

ANGLE FACING WEST
(WINDOW IN BACKGROUND)

ANGLE FACING EAST
(REVERSE ANGLE WITH
WALL IN BACKGROUND)

RED LOOKS BOTH WAYS,
THEN DOWN...

RED'S POV: ERNIE COMES
INTO VIEW WITH CART...

LOW ANGLE OF
ERNIE APPROACHING...

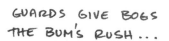

GUARDS GIVE BOGS
THE BUM'S RUSH...

...RIGHT OVER RAIL!

ANGLE LOOKING DOWN:
Red gazes up, then
whips out of frame!

RED POV: Bogs plummets
toward camera! (Actor
in harness on stunt rig.)

BOGS' POV: CAMERA ON
"DESCENDER RIG" FALLS
TOWARD RED, WHO WHIPS
OUT OF FRAME!

FALLING CAMERA POV
CONTINUES ALL THE WAY
DOWN TO CLEANING CART!
(SEPARATE SHOT FROM RED)

Here comes Ernie...

Sc. 69 thru 77

page 8

... and here comes
BOGS!

CRASH!

Cart goes
skidding!

CART SKIDS ACROSS
CELLBLOCK AS CONS
DIVE FOR COVER!

RED LOOKS DOWN, STUNNED.
(SAME ANGLE AS PAGE 4)

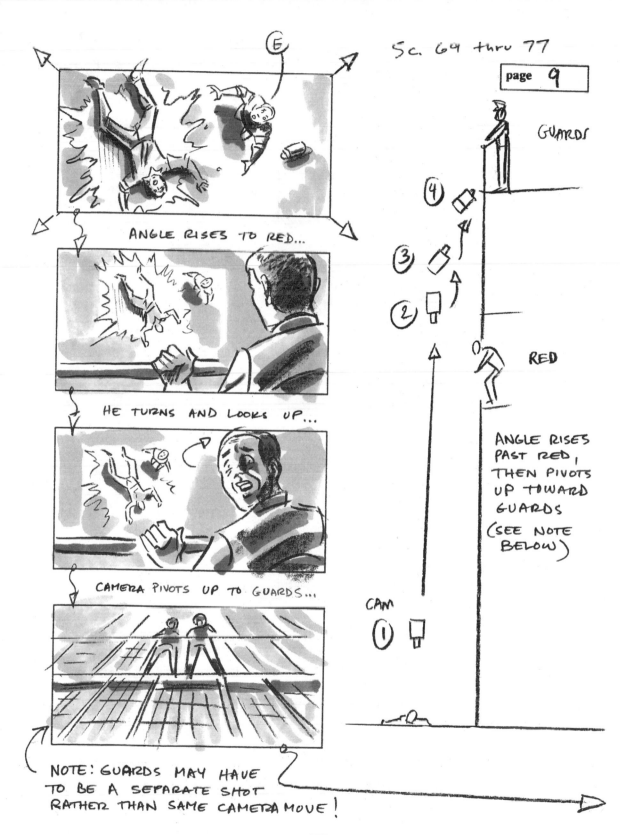

CONT'D

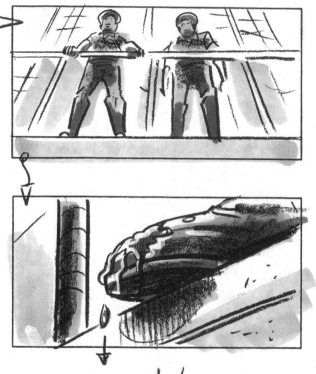

RISING TOWARD GUARDS
FOR DIALOGUE...

"DAMN, BYRON..."

PUSH IN ON HADLEY'S
SHOE. WE SEE DROP
OF BLOOD FALL...

...AND HIT RED'S CHEEK.

RED WIPES BLOOD OFF
AND LOOKS BACK DOWN AS
GUARDS AND CONS RUSH
TO BOGS.

END OF SEQUENCE

MEMO FROM THE TRENCHES
by Frank Darabont

"Memo from the Trenches" was originally published in 1995 in slightly altered form as a guest essay in David J. Schow's "Raving & Drooling" column for Fangoria magazine. (My thanks to Dave for inviting me to fill in for him.) I reprint it here in the hope that it might help inspire some budding screenwriters and filmmakers out there...

've had the great fortune of being a professional screenwriter (and, more recently, director) for going on ten years now. People often ask me what it's like doing what I do for a living—a fair enough question, but usually phrased with a tone suggesting that if I don't make it out to be as glamorous and fun as they think it ought to be, they're going to be damn disappointed. It's an interesting and rewarding life, one I wouldn't trade for anything—though I do have to admit in all candor that the day-to-day of it isn't nearly as much fun as I imagined when I was a kid dreaming of being in the movie business one day.

Not too long ago, I directed a movie based on Stephen King's novella *Rita Hayworth and Shawshank Redemption* from his book *Different Seasons* (one of King's best; check it out if you haven't already). It stars Tim Robbins and Morgan Freeman, plus a roster of dynamite actors that include Clancy Brown (a genre favorite for his roles as The Kurgan in *Highlander* and Frankenstein's monster in *The Bride*), *Die Hard II* tough guy Bill Sadler, bug-stompin' badass Mark Rolston from *Aliens*, and unsung national treasure James Whitmore (these days known mostly for his Miracle-Gro TV ads, but in my heart he'll always be the compassionate cop battling giant ants in *THEM!*, or the leader of the survivors marooned on a distant planet in Rod Serling's unforgettable *On Thursday We Leave for Home* episode of *Twilight Zone*). In the process of directing this film, I finally got to hang out with Stephen King after 14 years of knowing him only through phone calls and correspondence (he dropped by the editing room to watch a few reels, after which we shot the breeze over avocado-bacon-cheeseburgers at the Sundance Cafe), got to know and pick the brain of an extraordinary filmmaker named Rob Reiner (no stranger to King himself, having directed both *Stand By Me* and *Misery*—for my money the best big screen adaptations of King to date, along with Cronenberg's *The Dead Zone*), show my close-to-final cut to George Lucas for his critique (he liked the film a lot), and meet the likes of Barbra Streisand, Billy Crystal, Tom Cruise, Jack Nicholson, Arnold Schwarzenegger, and Susan Sarandon.

Okay, let's try something. Based on the above description, how many of you think what I do for a living sounds awfully glamorous and fun? C'mon, let's see those hands.

Okay, maybe it's a *little* glamorous, but only now that I have a moment to think back on it. Mostly it's a hell of a lot of hard work and precious little glitz of the sort that gets pounded down your throat by *Entertainment Tonight* or *E!* some 365 relentless days a year. Don't believe me? Let's try the flip-side of the job description: we began preproduction on *Shawshank* in January of 1993—casting, choosing locations, endless rounds of meetings with key technical people, you name it. My producer and I logged a lot of frequent-flier miles and racked up a lot of late nights chewing over the merits of this actor versus that (the only thing that made all those way-past-midnight sessions really worth it was that our casting director, Deborah Aquila, could make us laugh our asses off and vice versa—I swear, the later it got, the funnier we became). The prep phase went on for five months (three in Los Angeles, two on location in Ohio), at the end of which I was utterly exhausted. You've heard of the proverbial one-legged man in the ass-kicking contest? Well, prepping a film makes you feel like the guy whose ass *he* kicked.

Then the *real* work began. Three months of shooting in Mansfield, Ohio, working 15 to 18 hours a day, 6 days a week, with barely enough time to sit. And on Sunday (supposedly my day off), I sat around planning how to shoot the following week's scenes (doing homework, in other words). "Exhausting" is too wimpy a word to describe it—they have yet to *invent* a word that applies. You wind up in a sort of zombie-like daze, functioning on autopilot, reduced to putting one foot in front of the other like the kids in *The Long Walk* by Stephen King, the finish-line some mythical Promised Land you try not to think about lest you go mad with homesickness and despair, knowing that if you drop in your tracks they'll shoot you and leave you behind for the buzzards to chow down on. Sleep becomes a dim memory. The mental and physical stamina required is awesome. The stress is beyond belief.

But the last day of shooting *does* arrive. Congratulations, you've managed to slog through an eight-month endurance test of prepping and shooting that's left you reeling like a punch-drunk palooka who somehow went the distance in one of those old Warner Brothers boxing pictures. Ready to throw in the towel yet? Too bad, bucko! 'Cause hot on the heels of filming comes *postproduction,* which—while certainly kinder than what came before—is an endurance test all its own (we spent our last month of post working seven days a week on the final sound-mix: blending dialogue, music, and sound effects until our brains dribbled out our ears).

Okay, *now* how glamorous and fun does it sound?

Hmmm. I see fewer hands out there.

I once asked George Lucas why he hasn't directed in almost twenty years. His answer was that the job demands too much, takes too much out of you, and flat-out wears you down to nothing (and this coming from a man with the most tireless work-ethic I've ever seen). Having now directed, I see what he means. This film consumed nearly a year and a half of my life, friends, none of it glamorous and precious little of it fun, and all so some critic on TV can spend thirty seconds giving me a thumbs-up or thumbs-down. But here's what the critics *don't* know: the amazing thing about *any* movie is not whether it's good, but that it got made at all. *That's* amazing.

By now you're probably saying to yourself, *this Darabont sounds like an awful putz. Look at him, he gets to direct a major motion picture and all he does is complain. Is he looking for sympathy? A pat on the back? Sad songs played on violin?*

The answer is no to all of the above. I'm not seeking anything, I'm just telling you the day-to-day nature of what I do because some of you asked. Sympathy should be reserved for those who need it, not guys like me fortunate enough to have realized a life's dream. Nobody said it would be easy, and nobody promised it would be fun. I've gotten to do what I set out to do, and there is deep satisfaction in that. If you ask me, I'll tell you I'm one of the luckiest guys on the planet.

But if it's not glamorous and it's not fun, if it's nothing but gut-busting work, why do it?

Let me fill you in on a little secret. I think we've been sold a bill of goods in this country. We've been brainwashed into swallowing hook-line-and-sinker the spurious beer commercial dictum that "enjoyment" is the yardstick by which we should measure the worthiness of any endeavor—that anything worth doing must also by definition be "fun." Our standards of what we expect from ourselves have eroded. We've been MTV'ed and Nintendo'ed into oblivion, instantly gratified into complacency, and narcotized into junkiedom by the Home Shopping Network. Our icons are no longer the achievers of this world—the Einsteins, the Schweitzers, the Lindberghs—now we've got Bart Simpson and Beavis and Butt-head as role models who make underachieving seem not only okay, but "cool." No, I'm not one of those censorious loons who believes that Beavis and Butt-head are the root of all our ills and woes—I refuse to give them that much credit—but I seem to have less and less patience these days with things that celebrate and glamorize laziness and willful stupidity. Neither ignorance nor underachievement are badges of honor to wear with pride. Sadly, though, our "politically correct" society has come to believe that *nobody* should be made to feel stupid. Therefore, if Johnny can't read, let's not challenge him to learn—let's lower the educational standards in our schools so Johnny won't get his feelings hurt by being singled out as dumb. Swell idea— except that Johnny and his classmates will turn out to be just another lost genera- tion of functionally illiterate dickheads who won't be able to read their own diplomas if and when they graduate high school.

Sorry, folks, but I don't think our forefathers really had *"Party on, dude!"* in mind when they guaranteed the pursuit of happiness. Life doesn't come with a "fun war- ranty." We aren't issued E-tickets when we're born. Life is what we make of it, and the saddest loss is not to explore your potential within the short time you're given.

If this is beginning to sound like an inspirational sermon, there's a reason. Having now done a fair number of talks at colleges and universities, I've begun to realize that the one thing they don't teach in film school is how to believe in yourself. And yet, underlying the questions and answers that zip back and forth, I can always sense the *need* these students have to be reassured that their goals and ambitions—despite seeming so far out of reach—are attainable.

But it takes effort. If I'm any example, it took me nine years of starving, strug- gling, and honing my craft before I started making my living as a writer. Those were lean years, too, believe me. But in the nine years since then, I haven't *stopped* work- ing. I consider myself very lucky, but I also believe you *make* your own luck by applying the elbow-grease of determination and effort, by seizing every opportu- nity and nurturing a persistent belief in yourself no matter *how* bleak your chances seem (this philosophy lurks at the very heart of *The Shawshank Redemption*, and is one of the main reasons I fell in love with King's story). My standard joke—actu- ally, I'm fairly serious—is that there are potentially more talented writers and directors than I working in shoe stores and Burger Kings across the nation; the dif- ference is, I was willing to put in the nine years of effort and they weren't. More to the point, it took Thomas Edison a thousand attempts before he got that damn light bulb to turn on. Imagine if he'd gotten discouraged enough to quit after *only* nine hundred and ninety-nine tries.

The message here is simple, and John F. Kennedy said it best: "We choose to go to the moon not because it is easy, but because it is hard." Rough translation? If you have a dream, get up off your ass and start putting one foot in front of the other. Me, I'll take Edison and Kennedy over Beavis and Butt-head any old day.

CAST AND CREW CREDITS

Castle Rock Entertainment
presents
THE SHAWSHANK REDEMPTION

Andy Dufresne	Tim Robbins
Ellis Boyd "Red" Redding	Morgan Freeman
Warden Norton	Bob Gunton
Heywood	William Sadler
Captain Hadley	Clancy Brown
Tommy	Gil Bellows
Bogs Diamond	Mark Rolston
Brooks Hatlen	James Whitmore
1946 D.A.	Jeffrey DeMunn
Skeet	Larry Brandenburg
Jigger	Neil Giuntoli
Floyd	Brian Libby
Snooze	David Proval
Ernie	Joseph Ragno
Guard Mert	Jude Ciccolella
Guard Trout	Paul McCrane
Andy Dufresne's Wife	Renee Blaine
Glenn Quentin	Scott Mann
1946 Judge	John Horton
1947 Parole Hearings Man	Gordon C. Greene
Fresh Fish Con	Alfonso Freeman
Hungry Fish Con	V. J. Foster
New Fish Guard	John E. Summers
Fat Ass	Frank Medrano
Tyrell	Mack Miles
Laundry Bob	Alan R. Kessler
Laundry Truck Driver	Morgan Lund
Laundry Leonard	Cornell Wallace
Rooster	Gary Lee Davis
Pete	Neil Summers
Guard Youngblood	Ned Bellamy
Projectionist	Joseph Pecoraro
Hole Guard	Harold E. Cope, Jr.
Guard Dekins	Brian Delate
Guard Wiley	Don R. McManus
Moresby Batter	Donald E. Zinn
1954 Landlady	Dorothy Silver
1954 Food-Way Manager	Robert Haley
1954 Food-Way Woman	Dana Snyder
1957 Parole Hearings Man	John D. Craig
Ned Grimes	Ken Magee
Mail Caller	Eugene C. DePasquale
Elmo Blatch	Bill Bolender
Elderly Hole Guard	Ron Newell
Bullhorn Tower Guard	John R. Woodward
Man Missing Guard	Chuck Brauchler
Head Bull Haig	Dion Anderson
Bank Teller	Claire Slemmer
Bank Manager	James Kisicki
Bugle Editor	Rohn Thomas
1966 D.A.	Charlie Kearns
Duty Guard	Rob Reider
1967 Parole Hearings Man	Brian Brophy
1967 Food-Way Manager	Paul Kennedy

Directed by	Frank Darabont
Produced by	Niki Marvin
Screenplay by	Frank Darabont
Based on the Short Novel	
Rita Hayworth and	
Shawshank Redemption by	Stephen King
Executive Producers	Liz Glotzer
	David Lester
Director of Photography	Roger Deakins B.S.C.
Edited by	Richard Francis-Bruce
Production Designer	Terence Marsh
Costume Design by	Elizabeth McBride
Music by	Thomas Newman
Casting by	Deborah Aquila C.S.A.
Unit Production Manager	David Lester
First Assistant Director	John R. Woodward
Key Second Assistant Director	Thomas Schellenberg
Art Director	Peter Smith
Set Decorator	Michael Sierton
Production Supervisors	Kokayi Ampah
	Sue Bea Montgomery
Script Supervisors	Sioux Richards
	James Ellis
First Camera Assistants	Eric Swanek
	Robin Brown
Second Camera Assistants	Andy Harris
	Bill Nielsen Jr.
	Bobby Mancuso
Steadicam Operator	Gerrit Dangremond
Production Sound Mixer	Willie Burton

Boom Operator	Marvin Lewis
Cable Person	Kevin Boyd
Location Manager	Kokayi Ampah
2nd 2nd Assistant Director	Michael Greenwood
First Assistant Editor	Patty Galvin
Second Assistant Editor	Robert Lusted
Apprentice Editor	Jeff Canavan
Editorial Assistant	David Johnson
Casting Associate	Jane Shannon
Production Office Coordinator	Beth Hickman
Assistant Office Coordinator	Margaret Orlando
Office Assistant	Anne Hilbert
Office Intern	Amie Tschappat
Property Master	Tom Shaw
Gaffer	Bill O'Leary
Key Grip	Don Cerrone
Key Make-up Artist	Kevin Haney
Make-up Artists	Monty Westmore
	Jeni Lee Dinkel
Key Hairstylist	Phillip Ivey
Hairstylists	Roy Bryson
	Pamela Priest
Senior Set Designer	Antoinette Gordon
Set Designer	Joe Hodges
Storyboard Consultant	Peter Von Sholly
Special Effects	Bob Williams
Animal Trainer	Scott Hart
Additional Animal Wrangler	Therese Amadio
Assistant to Frank Darabont	Robert Barnett
Assistant to Niki Marvin	Sophia Xixis
Wardrobe Supervisor	Taneia Lednicky
Key Costumers	Mira Zavidowsky
	Kris Kearney
Costumers	Eva Prappas
	Donnie McFinely
Seamstress	Carol Buckler
Wardrobe Assistant	Cookie Beard
Construction Coordinator	Sebastian Milito
Transportation Coordinator	David Marder
Transportation Captain	Fred Culbertson
Stunt Coordinator	Jerry Gatlin
Construction Foreman	Dixwell Stillman
Production Accountant	Ramona Waggoner
Assistant Production Accountant	Jane Estocin
Accounting Assistants	Kelley Baker
	Michael Vasquez
	Karin Mercurio
Set Estimator	Susan Fraley
Assistant Art Director	Jack Evans
Decorating Consultant	Bobby Baker
Art Department Assistant	Rhonda Yeater
Still Photographer	Michael Weinstein
Unit Publicist	Ernie Malik
Publicity	Nancy Seltzer & Associates, Inc.
Video Assist	Van Scarboro
Video Assistant	Judy Scarboro

Ohio Casting	D. Lynn Meyer
Background Casting	Ivy Weiss
Casting Assistant	Julie Weiss
Background Casting Assistant	Brent Scarpo
Background Casting Intern	Adam Moyer
Lead Person	Alba Leone
On Set Dresser	Lee Baird
Set Dressers	Christopher Neely
	John M. Heuberger
	Jack Hering
Propman	Carey Harris
Best Boy Electric	Jeremy Knaster
Rigging Gaffer	Richie Ford
Rigging Best Boy	Tony Corapi
Lamp Operators	Bill Moore
	William Kingsley
	Ruben Turner
	Quincy Koenig
Electric Riggers	Joseph Short
	James Gribbins
Best Boy Grip	Keith Bunting
Rigging Grip	Charley Quinlivin
Second Rigging Grip	John Archibald
Dolly Grip	Bruce Hamme
Grips	Eugene DePasquale III
	Kenneth McCahan
	Russell Milner
	Brian Buzzelli
	Thomas Guidugli
	James Harrington
Rigging Grips	Rex Buckingham
	Jorgen Christensen
Film Loader	Hope Nielsen
First Aid	Frank McKeon
Stunt Players	Tom Morga
	Ben Scott
	Dan Barringer
	Mickey Guinn
	Dick Hancock
	Allen Michael Lerner
	Fred Culbertson
Lighting Stand-ins	James Burke
	Dexter Hammett
	Max Gerber
	David Gilby
	Tim Amstutz
	Bill Martin
	Jon Stinehour

Drivers

Chick Elwell	Ray Greene
Mickey Guinn	Chuck Ramsey
David Turner	Chip Vincent
William Culbertson	Douglas Miller
Ken Nevin Jr.	Scott Ruetenik
Harold Garnsey	Dick Furr

Drivers, cont.		Re-Recording Mixers.............................Robert J. Litt
David Smith	Ronald Hogle	Elliot Tyson
Judith Reed	Glen Murphy	Michael Herbick
James Graham	Tom Park	Mixing Recordists.......................................Jack Keller
J. D. Thomas	Robert Conrad	David Behle
William Davis	Sally Givens	Sound Editors...Bill Manger
Neil Knoff	Roland Maurer	Jeff Clark
Gary Mishey	Donald Snyder	Zack Davis

Dale Johnston

Larry Lester

Bruce Bell

Richard Oswald

Propmaker Foreman...................................Earl Betts
Propshop Foremen...........................Isadoro Raponi
             Jim Henry
Propmaker Gang Bosses....................Scott Mizgaites
             Chad Goodrich
Key Carpenter..Paul Wells
Plasterer...Glen Blanton
Labor Foreman.............................Barrett Fleetwood
Labor Gang Boss...................................John Barbera
Paint Foreman..Peter J. Allen
Paint Gang Bosses........................Robert Hawthorne
             James Hawthorne
Standby Painter.......................................Todd Hatfield
Painters...Blair Gibeau
             Kelley Collopy
Helicopter Pilot...............Robert "Bobby Z" Zajonc
Gyrosphere Operator...............................Mike Kelem
Gyrosphere Assistants.............................Ed Gutentag
             Richard Burton
Location Assistants..................................Scott Stahler
             Chris Cozzi
Set Production Assistants................David McQuade
             Jesse Johnson
Assistant to Tim Robbins.........................Tom Cotter
Assistant to Morgan Freeman..........Alfonso Freeman
Craft Services...Mark Moelter
             Don Speakman
             Brian Boggs
Caterer...Joe Schultz
             Carlos Garcia
             Jose Lopez
Post Production Sound..........Bald Eagle Sound, Inc.
Supervising Sound Editor....................John M. Stacy

ADR Supervisor..Petra Bach
ADR Editors..Robert Ulrich
             Shelley Rae Hinton
Assistant Sound Editors ....Lori Martino
             Bill Weinman
             Janelle Showalter
Foley Artists...Kevin Bartnof
             Ellen Heuer
Foley Mixer... Marilyn Graf
ADR Voice Casting............................. Barbara Harris
ADR Mixer.......................................Tom O'Connell
Additional ADR Mixers............................Paul Zydel
             Doc Kane
Foley Recordist.......................................Ron Grafton
ADR Recordist...Rick Canelli
Additional ADR Recordists............Michael Cerone
             Mike Boudry
Music Editor...Bill Bernstein
Assistant Music Editor......................James C. Makiej
Music Orchestrator..........................Thomas Pasatieri
Music Scoring Mixer..............................Dennis Sands
Music Contractor......................................Leslie Morris
Music Preparation.............................Julian Bratolyubov
Music Consultant..........Arlene Fishbach Enterprises
Titles and Opticals......................................Pacific Title
Color Timer...David Orr
Negative Cutter......................D. Bassett & Associates
Digital Special Effects......Motion Pixel Corporation

"If I Didn't Care" by Jack Lawrence, Performed by The Inkspots, Courtesy of MCA Records

"The Marriage of Figaro/Duettino—Sull'Aria" by Wolfgang Amadeus Mozart, Performed by Deutsche
Oper Berlin/Karl Böhm, Courtesy of Deutsche Grammophon, by arrangement with PolyGram Special Markets

"Put the Blame on Mame" by Allan Roberts and Doris Fisher

"Lovesick Blues" by Cliff Friend and Irving Mills, Performed by Hank Williams,
Courtesy of PolyGram Special Markets

"Willie and the Hand Jive," by Johnny Otis, Performed by The Johnny Otis Show, Courtesy of Capitol
Records under license from CEMA Special Markets

Frank Arpad Darabont was born in 1959 in Montcbeliard, France, the son of Hungarian refugees who had fled Budapest during the failed 1956 revolution. Brought to America while still a baby, Frank graduated from Hollywood High School in 1977 and began his film career as a production assistant on a low-budget 1980 horror movie called *Hell Night*. He spent the next six years working as a set dresser and in set construction while struggling to be a screenwriter. In 1986, people finally started paying Frank to write, which he's been gratefully doing ever since. He's also directed two films professionally during that time: a 1989 cable TV movie entitled *Buried Alive,* and his 1994 feature debut, *The Shawshank Redemption*. For his screenplay of *The Shawshank Redemption,* Frank won the USC Scripter Award (shared with Stephen King), the PEN Center USA West Award, and the Humanitas Prize—in addition to being nominated for an Academy Award, a Writers Guild Award, and a Golden Globe. He was also nominated as Best Director by the Directors Guild of America. He lives in Los Angeles.

Stephen Edwin King was born in 1947 in Portland, Maine, the second son of Donald and Nellie Ruth Pillsbury King. He attended the University of Maine at Orono, where he secured a B.S. in English that qualified him to teach at the high school level. He and Tabitha Spruce met while both students, and were married in 1971. That same year, Stephen began teaching English classes at a public high school in Hampden, Maine. His stunning writing career took off in 1973 with the publication of his first novel, *Carrie,* the success of which allowed him to leave teaching and pursue writing full-time. He has since become the best-selling author of all time with works such as *The Shining, Salem's Lot, The Stand, The Dead Zone,* and many subsequent works too numerous to mention here. His short novel, *Rita Hayworth and Shawshank Redemption,* published in 1982 in the book *Different Seasons,* became the basis for the 1994 Castle Rock film, *The Shawshank Redemption*. Stephen and Tabitha King live in Bangor, Maine, and have three children: Naomi Rachel, Joe Hill, and Owen Phillip.

The *Shawshank Redemption* was nominated for 7 Academy Awards in the following categories: Best Picture (Niki Marvin, producer, also nominated for a Producers Guild Award), Best Actor (Morgan Freeman, also nominated for a Screen Actors Guild Award and a Golden Globe), Best Screenplay Based on Material Previously Produced or Published (Frank Darabont, also nominated for a Writers Guild Award, a Golden Globe, and as Best Director by the Directors Guild of America), Best Cinematography (Roger Deakins, also nominated for and winner of the American Society of Cinematographers Award), Best Original Score (Thomas Newman, also nominated for a Grammy Award), Best Editing (Richard Francis-Bruce, also nominated for an American Cinema Editors Awards), and Best Sound (Robert J. Litt, Elliot Tyson, Michael Herbick, Willie Burton). Tim Robbins was nominated for a Screen Actors Guild Award as Best Actor.